Laughton Osborn

The Silver Head - The Double Deceit - Comedies

Laughton Osborn

The Silver Head - The Double Deceit - Comedies

ISBN/EAN: 9783744791960

Printed in Europe, USA, Canada, Australia, Japan

Cover: Foto ©Andreas Hilbeck / pixelio.de

More available books at **www.hansebooks.com**

THE SILVER HEAD

THE DOUBLE DECEIT

COMEDIES

BY

LAUGHTON OSBORN

NEW YORK
DOOLADY PUBLISHER
448 BROOME STREET
1867

THE SILVER HEAD

MDCCCXLV

CHARACTERS

SIR HENRY FERGUSON, *formerly a Colonel in the British Army, — having living with him the children of a deceased brother and sister, whom he has adopted.*

MANFRED,
OSCAR, } *his nephews, sons of his deceased brother.*

THEODORE VINCENT, *friend of Manfred.*

MARK MATTISON, *father of Helen.*

RICHARD, *his son.*

MEDDLEHAM, *a distant kinsman of the young Fergusons by their mother's side, and, in the same way, of the Mattisons.*

HELEN, *a poor girl, beloved of Manfred.*

SYBIL VERNON, *a young widow, orphan niece of Sir Henry, through a sister.*

SAFFISE, *a Creole from New Orleans; a casual acquaintance of Helen's, and, in secret, the mistress of Oscar Ferguson.*

———

SCENE. *Baltimore.*

TIME. *That occupied in the representation.*

THE SILVER HEAD

ACT THE FIRST

Scene I. A Parlor in the house of Sir Henry.

Enter, MANFRED *and* OSCAR.

Osc. Now, by my soul! — which, prais'd be Heaven! is not
Like yours, poetic and most righteous 'Fred,
Made of the willow, swaying with all winds,
Though 't were a breath too light the veil to crimple
· That wantons with the lips you dare not——

        Manf. Hush ! —
Yet is not broken by the strongest storm
That splits your heart of oak —

       Osc. Splits! Prythee, how ?
Feel here [*striking his breast.*] — 'T is not your mis-
 tress' breast — Now God
Forbid! you 'd faint if 't were — ha, ha! — Does this
      [*striking it again heartily.*
Sound like a riven heart, or, 'faith, like one

That anything is like to rive? — at least
Anything driven with a feather's impulse,
Like woman's pithless and unweighable love —
A woman's too, that——
               Manf. Brother Oscar, peace!
Your jests are scurril, and I like them not.
Osc. Prodigious! 'T is exceeding rare, no doubt,
For men to wince, when, edg'd to do them good,
The surgeon's scalpel — scurril would you call it?
Bites to the quick! eh!
             Manf. Well, well, well! Have done.
Your willows and your knives, prosaic sage,
Have swept and cut your purpose off.
                  Osc. That's true.
We come of a poetic race, you know;
Our grandsire rhym'd — as you do; but my vein
Is good sound satire, not a lover's whine.

          Enter VINCENT.

Vin. When satire serves to point the sting of spleen,
Or give an edge to envy, nobler far
It is, I deem, to be the weakest lover——
Osc. That splutters fustian when he's half seas over.—
There's a rhyme for you; and, as one can't be
Long in your presence or my brother's here,
And not be made to love the Muse, or muse,
I 'll give you, sir, another, which is this:
'T were folly to be wise, where folly 's bliss.
You 've heard the sense before; but, if you choose,

May have a variation : — thus it reads :

He most fears satire, who its lash most needs.

Manf. Brother ! — Dear Vincent ! Oscar, well you know——

Osc. Never likes meddling.

              Vinc. And so little likes

His brother's friend, that even his uncle's house

Is no protection from unmanner'd spleen.

                 [*Oscar bows low to Vincent.*

Manf. Peace ! you are both my friends [*taking a hand of*

              each] ; why should you jar ?

Osc. Because ——

        Manf. You rogue ! 't is but a trick, I see,

To put me by. Come on : what did you mean

By thanking Heaven your soul was not as mine ?

Osc. [*shrugging his shoulders.*] 'Faith, that it sav'd my feet

    from getting wet.

Vin. [*significantly.*] Truth without flaw, though in false

    quibbling set.

Osc. Did I not tell you, brother Manfred ? See !

   'Your presence is contagious. I 'll withdraw,

To — ponder well the *truth without a flaw.*

        [*with deep expression, looking full on Vincent,*

                  and bowing very low.

Manf. [*arresting him as he is going.*] Yes, but you don't

    escape me in this wise.

Since we all rhyme, why here the question lies :

        [*laughingly, — in a well-meant effort to keep*

                peace between O. and V.

What lacks to make the adjuration whole,

You even now began? "Now, by my soul!"—
'T was thus you swore, then talk'd about a " willow!"

Osc.   As the Moor's bride, ere fell on her the pillow.
[*Changing his manner.*] I 'll tell you, Manfred.   Thus
I would have said:
Now, by my soul, you are the veriest ass
That ever thistle brows'd for wholesome grain.
Occasion courts you, and you turn your back;
Love woos you, and you smite him on the cheek;
Like Duncan's doom'd assassin, in the play,
"Letting *I dare not* wait upon *I would.*"

Vin. Where Conscience says *I dare not,* and *I would*
Is Passion's voice, to fear 's the braver part.
Be, Manfred, still that honest ass, and prize
The lawful thistle more than stolen grain.

Osc. Sage maxim-dealer — maker you are not,
Or else past ages borrow'd from your books, —
I might have reckon'd on your tongue.   Enough!
Manfred, there 's Helen waits you, with her eyes
That light to opening Paradise; and here —
Is Solomon, whom moderns *Vincent* call. Now choose.
But, by my soul, which, I thank Heaven again
Melts not like yours, you 'd better quickly choose,
Ere I leap Eden for you!

                Manf. You dare not! —

Osc. Pshaw! *care* not; and Saffise contents me still.
I meant to play the Devil but for your good.

Vin. Manfred! [*sadly.*] I hope —— What is this Eve?

            Osc. [*biting his lips with vexation.*] Indeed!

Plague on 't! I thought this meddler knew. Good-
    day [*to Vin.*]:
Some day, sir, you and I may talk apart. [*retiring.*]
Vin. That 's as you please. [*Exit Oscar.*]
            Manf. Brother! for shame! — He 's gone.
You will not quarrel? [*anxiously to Vincent.*]
                    Promise me. [*taking both his hands.*]
                        ' *Vin.* Fear not:
Not of my will. But, Manfred, was this well?
A secret of such import? — Was my heart
Less fit to trust to? ——
                Manf. Than a brother's? No :
And your head fitter. Not to him — though well,
I deem, he loves me, [*Vin. shrugs his shoulders in-
        credulously. Manf. has his eyes cast down
        and does not observe the movement.*
            did I bare my heart:
He found my folly out I know not how.
And you — how could I brook your censure, face
Your laugh ?
            Vin. Can this be possible? [*taking gently his
                hand.*] *My laugh? [Manf.
            looks up frankly and confidingly.*
Manf. [*pressing his hand.*] Forgive me; I was wrong; I
        should remember
Your pleasantry is never for the sad,
Nor your wit pointed at your friends. And yet ——
                            [*hesitating.*

Vin. And yet?

Manf. Your rule of duty is so stern!
This folly, of a kind —— How grave you look!
Hear me at once: hear all.

                A few days back,
My cousin Vernon's period to mourn
For her dead lord expired, and she must needs,
So custom and our uncle will'd, do off
Her weeds of wo, to the last shade of black,
With each month lessening, fashion still had left them.
Most women of her station, figure, youth,
Would straight have driven to the gayest shrine
Of Fashion's gayest priestess, there to assume
Her votaries' newest mode; but not so she;
For Sybil is a glorious creature; though
She 'll jest by the hour, when her light-arm'd wit
Rides tilt with even your own, yet, like to you,
Within, where the world sees her not, there Duty
Rules like an empress, and admits no check.
One of Her laws is Charity, and Sybil
Would, where she can, make labor's wages just,
Quiting[1] the workman's product, not his name.
Vin. Noble! [*with emotion.*

     Manf. Is 't not? [*Looking at him attentively.*] Hence,
     for her new attire,
A poor girl has she working here at home,
At generous rates. 'T was in my cousin's rooms,
Where gallantry, my uncle's wishes more,
And true regard for Sybil, made me spend
Many glad hours, I first met this young maid.

Helen —— What makes you start?

      Vin. It is the name

Your brother mention'd.   Manfred ! —

      Manf. Do but hear.

Helen —— Hush ! hither come Sir Henry's self

And Sybil.   I am not in humor now

To meet them.   Let me go.   [*breaking from him.*

      Vin. For what? and whither?

Ah, Manfred !   [*Exit* MANFRED, *as*

      Enter

  SIR HENRY FERGUSON *and* SYBIL.

  Sir H. Has he left you all alone?

Syb. Without the fellowship of even his wits;

 For, uncle, see ! poor Mr. Vincent 's dumb.

Vin. Dumb with surprise his friend had power to fly

 The centre of attraction.

      Syb. O good sir,

My cousin is eccentric, well you know ;

The laws of vulgar planets rule not him.

Sir H. Well, let his orbit take him where it will,

 Here 's Mr. Vincent shall revolve with us.

 We 're for the flowers : to-day some rare ones bloom.

Vin. Whose beauty will grow lovelier in the light

 Of this contrasted ——

      Syb. Uncle, stop his speech ;

He makes the dullest compliments on earth.

Vin. For there 's a grace beyond the brightest powers ——

Syb. Is there?   Come then ; we 'll seek it in my flowers.

        [*Exeunt.*

SCENE II.

*A smaller room, or boudoir, very elegantly yet chastely fur-
nished, leading from the reception-room of Mrs. Vernon's
suite. The large door of communication, which directly
faces the spectators, is wide open, and, standing in the en-
trance, with his arms loosely folded, is seen* MANFRED, *
gazing pensively on* HELEN, *who is seated on a divan, before
a table, near the upper end of the room, or left² wing of the
scene, sewing. Various articles of needlework are on the
table before her, and on the divan beside her, where lies a
silk dress, partially made up. She does not appear aware
of* MANFRED'S *presence. He comes forward softly, and with
some timidity, yet without appearing to wish to escape notice. As he approaches,* HELEN *looks up, betrays emotion
and confusion, and, casting down her eyes, endeavors to
resume her work; but her embarrassment seems to set at
nought her efforts.*

Manf. I — I thought, Miss Helen ——

[*pausing in confusion.*

Hel. [*with an effort.*] Mrs. Vernon, sir,
Has just stepp'd out.

Manf. No doubt, will soon return.
I 'll wait her here [*taking a seat near the table; at
which Helen's embarrassment increases so evi-
dently, that he hastens to add — but his tone
is tender and timid, and perplexes her so
much that she lets fall her work.*
—— if 't will not hinder you.

Your work, Miss Helen. [*handing it respectfully. She
takes it with a mute motion of thanks, without
ever raising her eyes.*

                  Now, were I a judge,
I 'd think you 'd have me praise your gentle art.
There, see! your needle is unthreaded. Stay,
Let me essay; your fingers seem unsure. [*taking her
needle from her, which in her agitation she has
been unable to thread. She seems to have no
power of resistance or refusal.*
Are you not well? [*falteringly and with great tenderness.*

             You tremble. Ah! you work
Too steadily. So young, and so confin'd,
It is not well, believe me. There! you see
        [*drawing a thread through the eye of the needle.*
My hand is steadier than yours, though silk
And needles have not been my playthings.
    *He hands the needle, and in the act of her
taking it, which she does without raising her eyes,
their fingers touch. A deep silence,* HELEN *trying vainly to
use the needle,* MANFRED *gazing at her fixedly. —
Suddenly — springing up and clasping his
hands violently together.*

                        Oh!
This is pure madness! Helen! ——
                    Hel. O my God!
Sir, [*with a sudden effort.*] Mrs. Vernon —— You
will find her, sir,

In the conservatory with Sir Henry.

They went to see the blooming of the —— [*Gaining*
courage as she speaks, she ventures here to
look up, and meeting the impassioned gaze
of Manfred, stops short: her work falls
again — her eyes are cast down — her
breathing is audible.

Manf. What?

[*A pause, while he steadily regards her.*

Helen [*taking his seat beside her on the divan.*], to trifle
thus — to cheat ourselves —

Or try to, — for we cannot, — is waste torture.

Helen — dear Helen! — [*taking her hand. She makes*
a faint effort to withdraw it, and bursts into
tears.]   do not cry! [*staunching her*
tears with his own handkerchief.

to know

I love you — dearly, — can it be such pain?

[HELEN *suddenly disengages herself, and rises.*

Hel. You are — Sir Henry's nephew — and I am — [*again*
bursting into tears.

Manf. [*springing impetuously to her.*] Poor Helen Mattison [*mournfully.*]: and you are, too,

Pure Helen Mattison, and sweet, and good,

And beautiful as gentle; and I am —

Oh, very wicked thus to steal your heart!

For God has made me stronger, and I should

Have crush'd this dangerous feeling —— [*Hel. with-*
draws her hand, which he had retaken.

Hel. [*despairingly.*] Let me go.
Oh me! this house! what shall I do?
　　　　　　　　[*wringing her hands and weeping.*
　　　　　　　　　　　Manf. Ah yes!
Yes, yes, I am as mad as sinful.　Oh sit down!
　　　　　　　　[*leading her back to the divan.*
Resnme your work, your innocent work; wipe dry
Those bitter tears that I have made to flow.
There! there! be calm; I will withdraw; I'll meet
My consin and detain her —— 'T is too late!
I hear her coming.　[*Lowering his voice.*] Try, do try,
　　to sew.
　　He turns his back on her, and walks to the
open door, as SYBIL *enters.　She has a bunch of*
　　　　　flowers in her hand.
Syb.　You are wondrous dull, to be a wise man, Consin;
And as for seeking, trust me, never care
To Cupidize your eyes in blindman's-buff,—
They see as well unbandag'd.
　　　　　　　　Manf. I 'm at fault:
What mean you? [*He steals an uneasy glance at Helen.*
　　　　　Syb. Mean?　Why that you were at fault.
I, with Sir Henry, seek you, and you steal
Out of our sight, before our faces! then,
Go hunting for me, in the place I had left!
For I would swear you came not here to sew.
Bless us! how pale you look!　There [*giving him the*
　　　bunch of flowers.]; 't will revive you;
Though you deserve it not.　But are you ill?

Manf. O yes; the heat is stifling here.   Come out,
    The hour is fine for walking: the fresh air
    I think will do me good.   Do come! [*endeavoring to*
                                        lead her out.
                                Syb. The air?
Surely you dream: this room can not be close.
Sit down.   You naughty cousin! you have torn
My best flowers all to pieces!   And there, now!
You are mad! or getting so; you 're biting off
The heads of those you had left! [*taking the stock from*
                            him, and beating him with it.
                        Is 't my turn next?
Begone; or I shall scream for help. [*He does not pre-*
                tend to move, but gazes stealthily at Helen.
                            Indeed,
Sir Henry wants you, and your friend.   Do go;
You 'll find them in the billiard-room.
                                Manf. Yet Coz,
I would you 'd pity me, and come to walk.
Do now! [*endeavoring again to lead her from her seat.*
    Syb. And let you in a revery tear
My hair from out my head, or gnaw my hands!
No, sir, the mischief you 've done here will do: [*She*
        looks in her turn at Helen, but, in like man-
            ner, stealthily.
And 't is to pity you to send you off.
Besides, did you not hear? our uncle waits.
Manf. [*rising.*] You will not come?
                            Syb. No, flower-breaker, no!

Manf. Unkind! [*at the door.*

     Syb. Ah? Look at this. [*Pointing to the remains*
         of the nosegay.   He steals a look at Helen,
         and Exit,—Helen half lifting, timidly,
         her eyes a moment.   Sybil observes
         them both.

               Unkind, indeed!
And so they 'll bruise a heart, these men, like flowers,
Strip leaf by leaf off, in a pure abstraction,
And talk of kindness! [*Helen sighs.*] Is it so, my child?
Hel. Madam? — [*timidly, without lifting her eyes.*

     Syb. I ask'd you —— Heavens! what 's all this?
My silk you are sewing with white cotton, and
Your fingers drip with blood!   You prick them still!
Helen, what is the matter? [*in a kind tone, and taking*
         the work and needle from her hands.

             And these tears!
One on another, hot, upon my hands!
Hel. [*clasping her hands passionately, and looking up, as*
     if appealing to Heaven.

     O miserable me!   Why was I born!
Or why not born a lady, and born rich! [*lets fall her*
hands, and weeps bitterly.
Syb. [*taking her hand affectionately and speaking with*
     great kindness and in a tone of sympathy.

     Not born a lady? and born rich?   You mean,
I think, to ask, Why not without a heart.
For 't is your tenderness of heart, my girl,
Not want of wealth or station, makes you weep.

Yet you mean something. Come now, dry your eyes:
>
> [*Wiping Helen's tears with her handkerchief,*
> *just as Manfred had done before.*

Be calm, and speak.

Hel. O madam! I 'm not fit
That you should touch me thus with your own hands.

Syb. [*dropping her hand gently.*

Are you not pure then? honest-liv'd and chaste?

Hel. O yes, or could I sit beside you now?

Syb. [*taking her hand again.*] Why then,
What am I better than yourself, poor child,
Save that I have the means to do you good?

> [*Helen raises Sybil's fingers rapturously*
> *to her lips.*

No, no, not that! but this [*putting one arm about*
> *her.*] and this [*taking a hand*
> *in hers.*]— Now speak:

Fancy that Sybil Vernon is your friend,
And say, what would you, were you, Helen, born
A lady, and born rich?

> *Hel.* Born rich? a lady! [*in a low,*
> *half-murmured tone; then suddenly, in a sort*
> *of enthusiasm, while she drops Sybil's hand,*
> *who gazes on her with interest that be-*
> *comes admiration and wonder as she*
> *speaks.*

Why should I covet station, but for him?
That I might dare to look into his eyes,
And listen to his voice, nor dread his touch—

[*hesitating.*

Whose love I might be, were I born as high.

Why long for riches, lady, but to be

Able to pour them all into his lap?

I could not covet to be great myself,

But to make others greater than myself.

Syb. But why this? Why not love in your own sphere?

Hel. Madam, because I find there none to love.

Syb. I do believe you: for your thoughts, your words,

Your mien are, Helen, — not above your birth,

For that I know not, — but above the range

Their life allows the humble; they are those

Leisure, and gentle breeding, converse long

With the refin'd and delicate, chiefly give.

Still, nature, and a — proud love, may do much. [*look-*

ing at her closely.

Hel.   Ah madam, my romance has made you sport!

A girl's ambitious longings, a — a — sketch

Which Fancy color'd ——

                    Syb. Hush! be always true:

Hide what you will, but seek not to deceive.

Your picture was heart-painted. For my " sport "—

How long since I grew wicked in your eyes?

Or have you ever found me to forget

That gentle breeding which but now I prais'd?

Hel.   Oh madam, do forgive me! Who that knows

Aught of your ——

                    Syb. Prithee, praise not; but say on.

Whence then, if not from love and nature, came

That tone and air that make us equal?   Speak.

> [*taking her hand.   At first, Helen, by a sud-*
> *den and impetuous movement, raises Sybil's*
> *fingers to her lips, then she resigns her*
> *hand to her, and answers.*

Hel.   My father has them.   Ah, could you but see
His white head, with its venerable length
Of hair like an apostle's, as he reads
At nightfall in the leisure want allows.
The lore and poetry of other days,
Days when he was not happier perhaps,
But had more ease to cultivate such tastes,
You would not wonder, that a not rude heart,
And docile spirit that still sought to please
Where pleasing was both duty and delight,
Should catch some faint reflection from his blaze.

Syb. [*smiling, while she places the hand she has disengaged,*
caressingly on the head of Helen.]

> And I shall see him.

> > > *Hel.* Madam! — [*surprised.*

> > > > *Syb.* And why not?

Are we not friends?   To-morrow I shall call
At Helen's house; perhaps the good old man
Will not be loath to see his daughter's friend.
Come, don't be silly! [*putting the end of her fingers*
on Helen's lips.] And besides, my child,
You will not hither come again to work.

Hel. [*betraying herself in the extremity of her surprise and*
grief.] Oh God!

Syb. [*soothingly.*] Hush, Helen! you yourself
    shall own
To-morrow, there is cause, and I am right.
Be not abash'd, poor child! [*kissing her on the fore-
                    head.*
          Hel. [*hastily.*] No madam, I
Am only grateful.
          Syb. There now, get your things.
You shall not wait your brother, but go home
Before the night.   You are not well to work;
And those sweet eyes want resting : and, besides —
Besides —
Hel. [*firmly yet sadly.*] Besides, 't is better that I should.   ·
    O, would I never! ——
          . *Syb.* Nay, do not be rash.
How know you what I have to say, the morn?
Now we will part; but to my closet first,
To wash your secret from those telltale eyes.
Hel. [*despondingly.*] Thanks! but O madam, what shall
    wash it out
 From heart and brain!
Syb. [*putting her arm about Helen's waist, and pressing
    her to her.*] Time, Helen, and — my love.
    Exeunt, — Helen kissing Sybil's hand.

SCENE III.

As in Scene I. — MANFRED *and* VINCENT.

Manf. Now you know all. [*sadly.*
                    Vin. All, Manfred? Whence then came
The changes of your cheek, now flush'd, now pale,
Your tremulousness of hand, and wandering eye,
And still more absent mind — so gone, that when
Sir Henry ask'd you questions of our game,
You star'd so wildly stupid, that I look'd
To see him break his cue upon your head —
Whence came this? And whence came you? Ah, my
        friend!
Was it well done, to? —— But I will not chide you.
Say, only say, you did not tell your love.
Manf. Alas!
        Vin. Unhappy! — Yet not guilty, so
You did not from intention make it known.
Manf. No, on my honor, no!
                    Vin. I know it well.
Such baseness is not Manfred's, else 't were vain
To give you counsel or to urge you more.
And was this burst of passion welcome? [*anxious.*
                        Manf. No.
Oh yes it was! And yet it was not too.
She wept, yet trembled, sought to go, yet staid,
Withdrew her hand, yet through the delicate skin
I felt the hot blood bubble; then her breath,

That echo'd passionate sigh for sigh! her eyes,
That through their down-turn'd lashes, pour'd such rain
With fire mix'd! — [*Manfred has spoken with an en-*
thusiasm or transport increasing at every
clause, and now grasps Vincent's hands in
both of his.

Vin. Madman! Paint no more. Your eyes
Glow with unholy rapture, and your heart,
O Manfred! where is its remorse? Where now?

[*Manf. buries his face in his hands.*

This poor girl, this young virgin, whose weak heart
It is so easy, for a man like you,
To win, — as 't is to break it, you would not
Debauch her, Manfred?

Manf. Vincent!

Vin. Hush! 't is I,
I, Vincent, that have ask'd it, and I answer,
No, not even in your dreams. What would you then?
You would not, you, the accomplish'd and the learn'd,
The rich, the high in fashion as in name,
The darling of your uncle, who on you,
And not on Oscar, leans, as on the prop
And glory of his now declining years,
You would not, would you, Manfred Ferguson,
[*quickening his tone.*] You would not make your wife
of this poor girl?

Manf. No, no! [*mournfully.*

Vin. No; that proud old man, whose sense
Of honor is so nice, that he would curse you —

He, that was bred amid licentious wars,
And nurtur'd his high morals in a camp —
Were you to ruin this young innocent girl,
Yet, did his nephew wed her, do you think
This proud old man would bless you, Manfred? he?

Manf. O peace! No more: I 'll crush this passion.

                                               Vin. Yes.

For 't is not only kindred, friends, the world,
That you would alienate or sore offend
By such a marriage, but your very self.
What would her rude relations be to you?
Could you mix fairly with them, you, a man
So delicate and nice, so high-refin'd,
That the world deems you a voluptuary,
And I, who know you better, find in this —
Your passionate love of beauty of all kinds,
Your loathing of the coarse, the rude, the mean —
Senses so exquisite, that commonest things,
That pass unnotic'd by most delicate minds,
Give to you provocation, pain, disgust, —
Could you, this man, take by their horny hands
Her kindred, and endure their uncouth slang?

Manf. Death! I have told you, Vincent, I *will* break —
Though it should break my heart ——

                                       Vin. Not yours, nor hers.

Hearts are not made of such a glassy stuff.
They crack perhaps a little, but then time
Cements the portions, and the ruptur'd part,
Though in its seam unsightly, stands not less.

You will break off this passion — Well! at once?

Manf. At once. Oh yes!

> *He has walked in his excitement towards one end*
> *of the apartment, and, as he speaks, he seems*
> *to see something through a window, or other-*
> *wise. He starts and springs to his hat,*
> *which is lying on a table.*
>
> Ah! —
>
> *Vin.* Manfred! this your word!

Manf. [*struggling with him.*] But she is going! Vincent,
[*fiercely.*] let me go!

Vin. Never! What, are you Manfred? and a man?
Where is your promise, which is yet scarce cold?
Sit down. There? 't is all over. Courage! So!

Manf. [*who has allowed himself to be seated, throwing his*
head on Vincent's shoulder, who leans soothingly
over him.

Cruel! yet kind!

> *Vin.* Courageous you, and true.

The Drop descends.

Vol. IV.—2

Aot the Second.

Scene I.   The little parlor belonging to Saffise's lodgings.

OSCAR. SAFFISE.

Saff. And were you such a fool?

> *Osc.* I was, Miss Pert.

Saff. Then you may manage this affair yourself.

> I will not let my chambers, no, not I, [*saucily curtsy-*
> > *ing, spreading out her dress, and*
> > *strutting from him.*
>
> To help a fellow in his plot, so dull
> He makes his tongue a fingerpost, to show
> The world his private road!   A close one, you!

Osc.   Your chambers, hussy!   And who pays the rent?

> > [*drawing her back by her skirts.*

Saff. Why I!   I work for it, I 'm sure.

> > *Osc.* You work!

> Your lazy fingers would not earn the hair.
> That stuffs this pad you mount on your fat loins,
> To make a pismire of you, or a churn.

Saff. [*pouting.*] What ails my bustle? 't is n't on your
> back?

Osc.   No, 'faith! or I must needs cut off my skirts.

> But come, we will not quarrel: I but jested;
> This hand 's a pretty one — I like it well —
> And work would spoil 't.   Here, sit upon my knees.

Saff. Saucy!   I sha' n't do any such a thing.

Osc.   Sit, in the devil's name, then, where you please.

My brother's humor is strong on me to-day!

I shall turn rhymer some of these odd moons.

Saff. You 'd better turn an oysterman, and cry

Your ware as open as your mouth.

        Osc. Come, come,

You are getting too severe.   Don't mount my horse;

'T will throw you.   How was I, since you 're so wise,

To reckon on this sudden change of mood?

That hot-head fool, my brother, who still wears

His heart upon his lips, and ever blabs

His uppermost thought, as if the world were fill'd

With honest dreamers like himself——

        Saff. Did not,

Frank as you make him, tell this freak to you:

You found him out with Helen, or I help'd you.

Osc.   Why that is true. [*biting his nails from vexation.*

     I *was* an ass, to deem

He 'd prate, though loose of tongue, of an amour

To such a canting hypocrite as Vincent,

While I, who am not strict——

        Saff. No, devil take you!

Osc.   Was kept in the dark!   Now, what is to be done?

All I can say, *that* Vincent will unsay,

And Manfred still keeps pure. —

Saff. [*singing contemptuously.*] Fol, lol, de lay!

Osc.   What do you mean?

      Saff.. Why that you *are* "an ass."

Did you not tell me, Manfred's weakest point
Was to let others lead him by the nose?

Osc.   Yes, though a very sage among his books,
And brilliant in his talk, all that 's but *head;*
Ilis heart is weaker than a child's, and wax
To any pressure.

        Saff. Then you set your stamp
Upon it, when this Mr. Vincent 's done——

Osc.   And give it a new impress.   You improve.

Saff.   Perhaps I do.   No matter.   Then you said;
This heart, which is as simple as a child's,
Is yet as fiery —— Pray, what did you say?

Osc.   As Ætna.   Ay, a lava-tide, his blood.
Were 't not his proud refinement keeps him pure,
And moral sense, as he would name the check,
Manfred 's of such a mold his passions' strength
Would make him the most sensual of men.
How your eyes sparkle!

        Saff. Never mind my eyes:
If 't were my wish to step in Helen's shoes,
You could not hinder me.   Now let us see.
Why do you want to ruin this poor girl?

Osc.   You pity her? [*with great surprise.*

        Saff. Not I! my misery loves
To be in company.

        Osc. You are so keen,
I needs must trust you.   Know, my uncle's pet
Is Manfred and not Oscar. —

        Saff. All know that.

Osc. Peace! will you?— And my uncle's folly is
To hold a stainless name above pure gold.
Still more than him he loves our cousin Vernon;
And 't is his wish —[*confused.*] But that is not the thing.
     [*Saff. looks at him very sharply.*
Now, do you see? If Manfred's passions rule,
I am the gainer; for Sir Henry 's rich.

Saff. I see; more than you think: you say I am keen.
You hope to get at once the greater part
Of uncle's wealth and all of cousin's too.

OSCAR *makes a gesture of rage and vexation, and turns
from her to hide his emotion.*

But let me tell you, you shall find Saffise
More than your match, and this rich widow's bed
Shall not hold Oscar Ferguson, who 's mine.
Perhaps too, Helen would not come amiss,
With brother Manfred to bear all the blame?

Osc. Have you the devil in you? [*turning fiercely on her.*
          Saff. [*coldly.*] No; have you?

They gaze at one another a long moment, SAFFISE *with her
arms akimbo,* OSCAR *with his thumbs in his
waistcoat-armholes.*

Osc. [*bursting into a laugh.*] Saff., you 're a shrewd one, —
yet a fool withal.
Come, toss this womans-jealousy aside,
And aid me in my plans: I 'll make you rich.

Saff. Well, but remember! there shall be no match
'Twixt you and that proud lady?
                    Osc. Sure there sha' n't.

You foolish child!   D' you find that Oscar tires
As yet of these round arms, thy swelling loins [*putting*
          his right arm about her waist, while he takes
          with his left hand a hand of hers, and they
          walk up and down together.
(Despite the bustle), and those parted breasts,
Of that round head, this silken hair, those eyes,
Whose saucy light might blind a thousand Helens,
Though she of old were one (especially now
Hers must be clean gone from their sockets) — [*She*
          strikes him on the forehead.
                                   pshaw!
Can I not love, and have my joke as well?
I have seen men fondle lasses, pipe in mouth,
And they, the girls, took one with the other fair,
The smoke and the caress — those eyes, Saffise,
And these red lips that pout a juicier kiss [*kissing her.*
Than any cousin's —
Saff. [*turning aside, and making with her lips a move-*
          ment and sound of disgust and
          contempt.
          Whom you cannot kiss.
Have done with foolery. [*shaking him off.*]
                    You want these rooms?
Osc.   And Helen in them.   But in truth, you jade,
It does surprise me, Helen, who is not
Exactly of your sort ——
               Saff. But may be soon.
Osc.   Stuff! you mistake me.   I meant, who is not

In speech, in thoughts, in manners, like her class —
  [*She is about angrily to interrupt him: he claps*
    his hand on her mouth.
Don't be a fool! — that she, this gentle girl,
Should make a playmate of a slut like you.
Saff. [*mastering her emotion.*] And do you think I seem to
  her as now ?
I suit my manners, blackguard, to my friends.
Osc. Pshaw, pretty pouter! can't you take a jest?
Saff. Yes, but true things are sometimes said in jest,
  And you, who are always jesting, never jest
  Without a bitter malice that stings sore.
  If human snakes could kill, this well I know,
  I should have died of poison —
                          Osc. Long ago.
Ha, ha! — But there's a rattle in my tail :
Folk get out of my way. — But, not to make
A rattle of your tale, go on, and say,
What intimacy have you with this girl?
Saff. She knows me as a seamstress, like herself.
  Once only did she, when we work'd together,
  Visit me here; but I have often call'd
  On Helen —
            Osc. Ay, she has a brother.
                              Saff. Devil!
Take care — I may be even with you yet. —
The old musicplate-engraver likes me not,
I see that plain, but Helen treats me well.
Osc. And you have never talk'd to her of men?

Saff. D' you take me for a lunatic, or fool?
Girls do not talk, to innocence like hers,
Of anything that may commit themselves.

Osc. Hum!

    Saff. But you don't believe in innocence.

Osc. Not I! but Manfred does: one fool 's enough
In the family. — So, she takes Saffise to be? ——

Saff. Just what she is: what should she know of you?
And, but for you, I am as good as she.

Osc. Phe-ew! [*whistling.*

      Saff. I swear, I 'll strike you with my fist!

Osc. 'T would spoil that pretty hand I just now prais'd. —
Can you induce this Helen, prude or maid,
To visit you again?

          ·*Saff.* When?

                 Osc. Now — to-night —
Within an hour.

          Saff. Yes, so it be not dark:
Her father will not trust her out at night.

Osc. He is wise.

      Saff. What then?

             Osc. I 'll bring my brother here.

Saff. Ah!

    Osc. Don't be scar'd; he would not look at you. —
But this is likely? She will come?

             Saff. She will.

Osc. Then look to see us both here in an hour.
We 'll leave her with my brother here alone;
And, if he is wiser than I was with you, [*putting on*
                         his hat.

He is — different in blood. [*Exit, carelessly.*

        Saff. As in all else. [*looking after*
      him with an expression of strong contempt,
            mixed with anger.

Mean, dirty, spiteful, coxcomb half, half rogne!
"Not look on me!" you viper? That for you!

            [*snapping her fingers.*

      Re-enter OSCAR.

Osc. I interrupt you. You were praising me. Go on.
Saff. As you deserve. What brings you back?

           Osc. Just this.

If Helen do not come, make you a signal
Out of your window, whistle, cough, or sing, —
Or — snap your fingers, that will do as well —
Just as you practis'd now.

        Saff. Or, say I pour
A basin of nice soapsuds on your head?
Osc. Why that will answer too. We 'll not come in.
Good bye now, gentle dove, and don't forget.
"That for you!" [*snapping his fingers, as he retires.*
      Ha, ha, ha! [*Exit.*

        Saff. I 'll hear you go. —
      [*holding the door ajar and listening.*
At last! [*slamming it.*
    —I have known a Creole, like myself,
That in New Orleans would have stabb'd you dead,
For half you have said to me. But I 'll do more.
You 'll not come in? Yes, but you shall: I 'll see

Whether this Manfred will *not look on me.*
Sharp as you are, you did but half pierce through
My secret — or car'd not to go so deep —
For daring is your sole virtue.   But for that,
I would not touch you with this old worn shoe. [*kick-
                    ing it violently off her foot.*
You shall not get your cousin, nor shall he [*throwing
                    herself on a couch.*
Keep Helen, — though, for I do hate the minx!
He shall, if he will, make her (*there* I 'll help him)
Just what his cursed brother has made me.
Then I will make him loathe her, silly thing,
With her dull eyes that would not scare a flea!
The noble fellow! he shall love a girl
With blood as fiery as his own, — that 's mine!
And fling her off, as I would my old shoe. [*kicking off
                    the other, with like force of action.*
As my old shoe! [*singing wildly.*
            as my old shoe! [*same.*
        [*Crying violently.*] Oh God!
I would I were a shoe! the poorest shoe
On the meanest foot in the world, I do, I do!
Then I should have no feeling of the foot
That trod me in the dirt — nor of that dirt! [*sobbing
                    hysterically.*
    Scene closes.

Scene II.

The humble parlor of Mark Mattison.

The old man is seated at a table reading in a small book.
HELEN *behind him, leaning over his shoulder.*

Hel. Repeat those lines, my father.
                            Matt. Gladly, child.

Reading.] As sensual passion sinks us to the ground,
    So a true love exalts us to the skies:
    All that God gives of pure and holy lies
    Within the verge of its enchanted round.
        Though low the object, yet shall there be found,
    In love, the charm to raise it in thine eyes.
    But oh, too froward youth, if thou be wise,
    Let no mean reach thy aspirations bound!
        Dare to love high above thee! so thy aim
    Shall lift thy soul to equal its desire,
    And make even failure glory and not shame,
        All thy heart's ore refined by the fire
    Of the proud altar where thy prayers aspire,
    And gilt by its reflection even thy name.

Hel. [*repeating slowly, and in a low tone.*
    " Dare to love high above thee "—— Was't well said ?
Matt. I thought so once, my daughter, and do still.
    How is this? the leaf is blister'd with your tears !
    What ails my child! Why should this make her
        weep ?

Hel. He was a noble spirit that thus wrote!
What was his name?

                Matt. Mark Mattison, they say.

Hel. Not you, my father? [*eagerly.*

                Matt. As I was in youth.

Matt. And men receiv'd your great thoughts? —

                Matt. With neglect.

It is the fate of better bards than I.

Hel. While senseless pens win competence and fame!
O me, my father, I was very weak
To grieve for want of riches! [*kissing his silver hair.*

                Matt. Helen — child!

I never knew you to repine before? [*inquiringly.*

Hel. I never did, till —— Father, did you mean —
        [*hesitatingly, and hiding her face on
                    his shoulder.*

'T is better to love hopelessly above one,
Where the affection is sincere and pure,
Than to —— I am very silly — do not mind me.
                    [*sobbing.*

Matt. Very unhappy, Helen, much I fear.
But let me answer your half-question first;
Then I have one myself to put in turn.—
Not better for one's peace perhaps and ease,
But better for high thoughts, for all that lifts
The soul above the prose of vulgar life.
For from affliction only God has will'd
The mind should take to it its angel-wings,
Whose feathers are weigh'd down and earthy made

By the slow-gathering dust of happy ease.
Fruition feeds the sense to starve the mind,
And dull inaction makes the stagnant pool,
Where storms rage not, but freshness neither plays,
Nor beauty smiles, as in the dimpled wave.
They who aspire, in love, as in all else,
In disappointment purge from dross their souls,
And gain by self-denial strength like gods. —
Such is my comment. And now tell me, child,
What is a hopeless, high-plac'd love to you?

HELEN, *who has lifted her head-and listened with eagerness*
and awakened spirit till now, here lets it sink
again upon the old man's shoulder.

Why have you wept? Why are you weeping now?
Why came you home so pale and thoughtful-sad?
Why for this week past have your cheeks grown thin?
Why do I hear you, through my chamber-wall,
Moan in your sleep, and, when the morning comes,
Find your eyes swollen with the trace of tears?
Why, in one word, has Helen, in one week,
Grown up a woman from a simple child?
Look up, my daughter, and now tell me why
You put that question to a man like me?
Have you —— [*his voice slightly agitated*]
          God help us! — has your work, my child,
Led you to Colonel Ferguson's too oft?

Hel. [*throwing herself at his knees and burying her face in*
his lap and weeping bitterly.
     Father, forgive me!

Matt. Helen! and for what?
You have not sinn'd, or you would never dare
To kiss my hands thus and embrace my knees.
Hel. O no, no! but I am unhappy.

      Matt. Yes.

Which is it? [*very brief pause.*]

    'T is not Oscar? [*anxiously.*

Hel. [*eagerly raising her head.*] Heavens, no!
Matt. Manfred— Ah! how you tremble! hapless child!
This is indeed a high and hopeless love!—
Manfred the world speaks well of,—and well speaks;
But he is lofty, his proud uncle's heir,
And—and—they say—his cousin Vernon——

        Hel. No!

    [*springing up, and folding her arms wildly*
      round the old man.

Father, you kill me! do not say so! no!
No, no, no! he does not love her!

      Matt: Ah! [*anxiously.*

Does he love *you*, my daughter! Has he dar'd?——

HELEN, *for answer, hugs him passionately, and kisses*
him again and again on cheek and brow,— then
leans her head on his shoulder.

But he is honorable; and absence—time——
My child, you must return there never more. [*passing*
      his hand soothingly over her hair.

Hel. Never more, father! [*sadly.*] Oh I never shall!
That lady too—so good like him, and true—

She bade me not return.

                   Matt. She knows it then?

Hel. I fear so; but she only said, the while

  She kiss'd me like a sister, call'd me friend,

  That on the morrow she would visit *you* ——

Matt. Me? Are you not deceiv'd? And yet I hope ——

Hel. These were her words: "To-morrow I shall call

  At Helen's house; perhaps the good old man

  Will not be loath to see his daughter's friend."

Matt. Bless, bless her, God! my child may yet be sav'd. —

  Go now, and dry your tears, and gain composure.

  Your brother must not know ——

                    Hel. Oh no! oh no! —

  But first, your pardon, father. [*kneeling at his feet.*

Matt. [*raising and kissing her.*] Mine, my child!

  'T is I should rather ask the like of thee.

  Is it your fault your nerves are not of steel,

  Your blood not torpid, and these sunny locks

  Not silver like your father's? Hush! he comes.

  Go to your room.   [*Exit* HELEN, *and*

       Enter RICHARD MATTISON.

          Rich. So Helen has got home? [*looking*
                      at the door where she has
                           disappeared.

I stopp'd an hour earlier than my wont,

And found her gone. I hope it is for good.

Matt. Why so, my son?

Rich. O sir, perhaps there 's cause
To fear she may have been there once too oft. ,
Matt. Sir, sir! for shame!

       Rich. Shame it may be, for all.
I 'll tell you. As I left the accursed house——
Matt. You forget, Richard. [*gravely and with dignity.*

       Rich. [*carelessly.*] Pardon, but I 'm warm.
Matt. That you are always.

       Rich. Well, well, 't is my blood.
I met, then, Mr. Ferguson. —

       Matt. [*hastily.*] Not Manfred?

       Rich. No;
Not that proud jackanapes; the younger man.
Matt. He does not please me.

       Rich. Nor the other me.
Yet neither of us knows them, save by name
And sight. He stopp'd me short, told who he was,
And said he knew of danger to my sister.
Matt. Ah!

Rich. I grew angry; but he check'd me straight,
Boldly, as one who knew that he was right. —
Matt. Boldly, as one who felt he was a man.
Say that, and you say all, I fear, you should.
Rich. It may be so; but he is frank and rough,
Talks as a freeman should, nor picks his words,
As who would say, "Mark! I am gentle-born,"
Like his more handsome brother.

       Matt. Have a care,
And trust an old man's and a father's word.

If all 's not gold that glitters, neither, son,
Is all true steel that has the temper'd look
And close grain of the fin'd and coal-burn'd iron.
Rich. Well, well! [*walking up and down.*
       Matt. Impatient boy! one day! [*holding his
       finger up warningly.*] —— Proceed:
And in few words.
       Rich. The fewer please me best.
I promis'd I would meet him in an hour,
In an appointed place which he propos'd,
And learn this danger. Then I hasten'd home
To see if Helen had not loiter'd, firm
That she shall not return, if you approve,
To any more such labor done abroad,
And with new rage, to think she might have spar'd
Herself and me and those white hairs this shame.
Matt. There is no shame, will never be from her!
Rich. Shall never be, I hope; but there is shame
In this mere speech about her, and her pride
Has been the cause of all. Did I not pray,
Pray as a beggar, she would let my toil
Support us both?
       Matt. No; if it was a prayer,
It was the most passionate one I ever heard.
But your intent was good. Yet blame not her:
'T was worthy of your sister and my child,
Not to live idle, when our common means
Scarcely suffice us for our common wants.
But who is that?

Rich. [*joyfully.*] Saffise. I know her step.

         [*moving eagerly to the door.*

Matt. I like her not, my son.

     Rich. [*softly.*] Hush! She is here.

As he opens the door, the scene closes.

SCENE III.

Same as in Act I. Sc. I.

MANFRED *alone, seated in an attitude of great dejection.*

Enter SYBIL.

Syb. What, cousin, still *pensoso?* still *amort?*

         [*Manf. rises.*

But you shall break no more *bouquets* for me.

I would as soon entrust you with my heart.

Manf. And 't were a perilous trust, my lady gay,

         [*with a forced smile.*

To one who never knew to keep his own.

       [*Resumes again his abstracted air.*

Syb. Yet I will wager half the greenhouse-yield,

You never treat it as you did my flowers.
Perhaps that kindness is for tenderer hearts.
Manf. Perhaps it is.
    Syb. Perhaps it is? And said,
As if you were confessing to the priest!
I was in hopes, but now, the gracious dawn
Of my fair presence had arous'd your brain;
But the dull sluggard turns, and sleeps again.
Manf. Excuse me, cousin Vernon, but I 'm sad,
And cannot bandy wit with you to-day.
Syb. And has not cousin Vernon then a heart,
That can be sad with Manfred, if he will?
Try her.
  Manf. And gladly, were it but a grief
That she might share.
     Syb. How know you, till you try?
Or is it that you deem my soul too light
Because I jest by the hour? See me now;
I am, my cousin, quite as sad as you,
And truly so, and solely for your sake.
Manf. You are a noble creature! [*seizing her hand.*
       Would to God! ——
Syb. Hush! let your brother talk that way: from you
I need no flattery, for you are true.
Sit down now, Manfred; let me sit by you,
And let me go back where I just began, —
But sadly, not in jest. The flowers you broke
Were such a natural emblem of man's love,
At least for the too-confiding of our sex,

Or weak and evil-guided, that I made
One of them on the spot, and spoke it out
For Helen's profit. [*Manf. starts.   She looks at him*
in silence.

    Manf. Helen!   And she? ——

       Syb. Wept.

Manf. Poor Helen! [*half unconsciously.*

    Syb. Poor indeed! that in the world
Had nothing but a heart to call her own,
And, being generous, gave it all away.

Manf. [*vehemently moved.*] Sybil! what mean you?
     Recovering.] What is that to me?

Syb. Oh! but I thought that you, whose heart is good,
And feels spontaneously, like a god's,
All human sorrow, would have griev'd to hear
Of such a gentle creature so distress'd, —
A girl so guileless, that her inmost soul
Is visible as her lips, so loving too,
That fondness wakes in her for being ask'd.

Manf. [*musingly.*] True—true! — and very beautiful! —
 her voice
The sweetest, save your own, I ever heard.

Syb. It is a hard fate for an humble girl,
With such a soul as this poor seamstress owns,
To see, as happier, richer women see,
Hear with like voice, and feel with sense as keen,
The tempter Love, and have no other choice,
Than to forego his ecstasies, or pay
With shame and ruin every thrill and sigh.

Manf. Sybil!—you torture me. [*in a very low voice.*

             Syb. I must, to heal. [*softly.*

Cousin, you are a man, in form and mien,
Fram'd of the kind, not to make woman false,
As says the playbook, but to keep them frail.
When everywhere around you where you move
You see the best among us, and most proud,
Eager to catch your glances, and the hearts
Of the more youthful, to whom love is new,
Flutter with pleasure at your mere approach,
Is it to be expected a poor girl,
Such as is Helen, should be more unmov'd?
That pressure of your fingers tells me, cousin,
You know it is in kindness that I pain you.
Oh it were very wicked in us both,
If Helen ever should come here again,
Or you go near to her! [*He makes a movement of pain-*
    ful surprise.]   Now, do not speak:
But promise me who, as you often say,
And truly, know you better than all else,
Save one alone, and know you to hold dear,
Promise you will exert your generous soul
To curb this passion; and to time and me
Leave Helen's cure.

        Manf. I will; for you and Vincent
Are truly friends, who dare to give me pain,
And punish me, like Heaven, to do me good.
But do—be kind to Helen.

            Syb. Kind? I love the girl,

Have vow'd to be her friend — her mate, I mean,
Not patroness, — and friend I will be.

Manf. [*in extremity of astonishment.*] You?
You peerless creature! [*kissing her hand rapturously.*
                              Where shall be the man
That shall deserve you!

                    Syb. Truth, coz, he must be
A different man from you.   I should not choose
To play the game of life with such a knave
Of hearts as you.

                    Manf. No, a more sober suit [*assuming a
                              little of her gayety.*
Is like to win more points.   I know of one. [*signifi-
                cantly, while Sybil endeavors, by rising, to
                conceal confusion.*

Syb.   Our talk is done in time: there's Cato coming
With his crook'd legs, to call us both to dine.
Let us spare his studies on the Line of Beauty.

Manf. Be gay; for you deserve it. [*Reaching his hand to her.*
       Syb. [*as she takes it.*] And be true
To your own self; and who more gay than you?

                              [*Exeunt, hand in hand.*

ACT THE THIRD

SCENE I. *Manfred's Study.*

*The furniture indicates the character of the owner's mind ;
everything being rather elegant than costly, and rather
costly than fine. A table in the centre covered with
books, drawings, music, etc. In various parts of the
room, books, musical instruments, pictures, copies of
antique vases, statuettes, etc. Among the latter, are con-
spicuous — the group of the Graces, the Venus of the
Medici, the (so called) Antinous, and the Laocoon.*

Enter OSCAR.

Osc. I wonder he has appetite to dine.
Till his return, I 'll have my talk with you,
Meet emblems of your owner's showy parts. [*taking
off his hat and bowing with mock reverence
to the objects round the room. He then
bows, in the same manner, to each par-
ticular cast as he addresses it.*
You, faultless three, [*to the Graces.*] whose delicate
· outline bears
The unmistakable charm of yet green youth,
Are symbols of my brother's classic taste,
And the fine sensualism which he would term

Voluptuous love of beauty.   I salute, [to the Venus.
Madam, in your immaculate limbs, his lust,
Veil'd with a simulate pudency as yours.
In thee, thou melancholy minion-boy! [to the Antinous.
His hero-grace, as cousin Vernon calls it.
Sweet liar!   But ah, before thy mass I bow,
                                  [to the Laocoon.
Thou double type of Manfred's self and me!
I am the snake, that round those muscular limbs,
And body's writhing trunk, shall twine, and twine —
In spirit, or the laws might make me hang —
Till little is left for uncle to admire. —
The gods and godlike of the place saluted,
Let 's see what 's on the table to adore.
Why this is good! [bending over a book.
                    H, E, — here 's Helen's name
Writ on this leaf of Dante!   Here 's her nose!
And hair, and scallop'd lips, and girlish cheeks!
But these are not her eyes.   The lovesick youth
Doubtless could never long enough gaze there,
To catch the physical shape would make them hers.
Drawn on his rarest copy! [looking at the title-page
          of the book.] — on the page
Which tells Francesca's very innocent love!
By your good leave I 'll trace a comment here.
Takes up a leadpencil from the table, and musing a
          brief moment writes on the page.
There, that will sting him. — Yes, 't is Helen's face,
                    [contemplating the page again.

Done *con amore*, with an artist's touch.

These lips! I mean to touch their freshness too;

But 't is not with a Brookman's lead I 'll do it.

And here 's again her name — writ once, twice o'er.

Why this is capital! [*aloud.*

Enter MANFRED.

    Manf. What is so?

        Osc. ²This, [*indicating the*

             leaf with his finger.

Where Dante takes the pains, in black and white,

To show the pretty seamstress tickles still.

But have you din'd already?

        Manf. Yes, I am ill.

But Vincent's spirits make me little miss'd.

And you?

    Osc. Too late, — must make the pantry serve.

Besides, your friend 's a side-dish rather stale:

I like no warm'd-up hashes at my meals.

Nor do I see that you digest him quite.

Manf. How so? [*with surprise.*

    Osc. [*looking down on the book.*

      H, E, L, Hel, — E, N, en; Helen:

That 's Helen's name I think that 's written here.

And this is Helen's pretty face as well.

Not much of Vincent in all this, I think.

Don't sigh, man: Vincent is a fool; and you —

Look at that figure [*pointing to the Venus.* —

      — and now gaze on these. [*the Graces.*

Can all the musty maxims of your friend
Give dreams like these? or is the waking sense
Of flesh and blood made in that image less
                              [*pointing again to the Venus.*
Than a prude's proverbs or a cold friend's cant?
Enjoy your fortune, or let some one else.

Manf. Oscar! — [*biting his lips with anger.*

     Osc. Frown, if you will; but to my sense
A seamstress and the friend of my Saffise
Seems scarce entitled to such grave respect.

Manf. What do you say! a friend of —— [*seizing his arm.*
    Osc. [*with distinctness, emphasizing each word.*
                  My fair friend.

No doubt they have rare sport at your expense,
When, meeting in the evening, Helen tells
How you have made a goddess of her, when
She was so willing to be thought a girl!

Manf. Stop, sir! I am choking! This is your foul tongue.

Osc. Ah? I must look: you have no mirror here?
              [*affecting to look about him.*
I really thought, this morning, it look'd clean.
Brother, stop in your turn! your walk, I mean,
And beating of your forehead like a fool.
Now let me ask you one plain question: this;
Have you not ever in boyhood, when your nose
Was in our mother's applebarrels, observ'd
How the bad fruit soon rotted all the sound
By merely lying next it? Well, I say
 Saffise is a bad woman, and her friend

Is Helen Mattison, your saintly maid.

Manf. Prove it!

   Osc. I swear it!

     Manf. Prove it! [*grasping his wrist.*

      Osc. And I will.

You shall, this very minute if you like,

Put your own questions to the Creole; nay,

'T is ten to one, what will be proof complete,

You 'll find your angel merry in her rooms.

And if you do, I hope you will not pray?

Manf. Don't mock me, Oscar; it is sore to find

One's dream of virtue a mere ——

     Osc. Fiddlestick!

Whoever dreamt of virtue in these girls,

But such a dreamer by wholesale as you!

Come, are you ready?

    Manf. In five minutes, yes.

Wait for me here. [*going out impetuously. Stops sud-*

  denly.] Ah now I do recall, [*turning round.*

I promis'd I would not seek out this girl.

Osc. And who desires you to? I am sure not I!

You merely go to chat with bright Saffise;

And that you owe to me, to prove my truth.

If ten to one your angel will be there,

Why one to ten she 'll not. But, if she be,

I hope again, for your own manhood's name,

You will not make a goddess of a — girl.

Go now, make haste; you 'll find me in the hall.

      [*Exit Manf.*

For were I, weathercock, to wait you here,
Some other wind might come to drive you back.
As he prepares to go out, hat in hand.

Enter VINCENT *and* SYBIL.

And here blow too; sou' westers, by the mass.
Syb.   Oscar! — We thought to find your brother here.
Osc.   And so did I; but here, you see, he is not.
I 'll go and seek him if you like, and say,
That Parson Vincent is about to pray. [*Exit Oscar.*
Syb.   Ha, ha! But Oscar, [*calling after him.*] Uncle ask'd
for you. —
You 'd think he fear'd impressment for the clerk!
Shall we proceed without him? Which of these
                    [*looking round her at the statuettes.*
Divinities deserves your office first?
Vin. [*bowing gallantly.*] That which has enter'd in the
temple last.
Syb.   I am congregation then, and idol too.
Begin, good father; lo the missal spread. [*taking up*
                                        the Dante.
But what is this? a desecrated page!
And here is Helen's name — and face! Alas!
The arrow was well-barb'd. And verses too!
Oh! this is Oscar's malice. Look there, sir.
                    [*handing the book to Vin.*
Vin. [*reading.*
'   Proud man! thus, on the tale of Frances' woes,
To write your Helen's name! for Dante shows,

His dame, though marry'd, found a page to woo her,
But yours has nothing else that can undo her.

Malice indeed, with subtle purpose too ;
For Virtue often wavers at a laugh.
Syb.   'T is as I judg'd, from Manfred's words, — you know
My cousin's peril ?
                         Vin. Only since this hour.
Syb. We will speak more of it.   As for this blow,
It shall not reach him. [*Takes up a bit of rubber from
                    the table, and procceds to erase the rhymes.*
              Vin. Generous creature ! — Pardon.
                                        [*in confusion.*
O that your cousin us'd my eyes to see!
Syb.   What ? that his brother is a heartless rake,
Who makes all honest feelings theme of jest?
Vin. Yet with not less of venom, that he jests.
No, I was more presumptuous in my thoughts,
And wonder'd at a blindness more complete,
At least less natural. [*He looks at her with much ear-
              nestness, and Syb. for a moment seems abashed.*
              Syb. Really, in this room [*assuming
                                        sprightliness.*
There must be some infection ! for I see
As dimly now as Manfred ; or you talk
Too darkly, 't may be, for my womans-sense.
You shall wait cousin Manfred here alone ; [*going.*
One blind is quite enough at once to cure.
*She comes back, and in a more natural manner, extending
              her hand frankly to Vincent:*

Dear Mr. Vincent, all depends on you:
Promise you will not, while this danger lasts,
Leave Manfred to himself.

Vin. [at first seems as if he would kiss the
hand he has taken, but only
bows over it.

No, on my soul!

[*Exit Sybil.*

Ah, little do you know that Vincent has
To battle with two enemies, and shield
His friend not only, but himself as well!
Conquest how glorious! victory over self;
And, for the generous Manfred, won —— ah me!
The noblest creature ever yet the heavens
Shed light on — and, I think, the fairest.   Strange!
Most strange indeed, a man so keenly quick'
To the perception of all beautiful forms,
The very atmosphere of whose study [*looking around*
him.] breathes
Exquisite tastes, and passions well refin'd,
A man of such romantic virtues too,
Should have preferr'd, to her —— But let me see.

[*taking up the Dante and looking*
at it attentively.

If this be Helen's face, and truly drawn,
'T is very sweet: but not more so than hers.
And then, her generous qualities! which oft
He makes his theme of praise ; too oft perhaps,
Since I have learn'd to muse on them so much.

I 'll question him of this.   But where is he? [*looking
toward the door, then relapsing into self-commu-
nion again.* .
She must have lov'd him, had he sought her love:
And it is right he should, — both right and best.
Sighing.] My fingers thrill yet with her touch. — My God!
Let me not, while I seek from Manfred's eyes
To pluck the mote, grow very blind myself!—
Queen of the Passions! [*apostrophizing the Venus.*
　　　　　　　　　　　still thy natural sway
Makes man forget his honor! —   No, not so!
Reason shall aid him, where not willing-weak,
Nor conscience torpid by a long neglect. —
I 'll seek this loiterer. —   What a soft, small hand!
　　　　　　　　　　　　　　[*sighing.*
Manfred, where art thou?
　　In a melancholy tone.] Why wast thou away?
　　　　　　　　　　　　　　　　[*Exit.*

SCENE II.

Saffise's parlor — As in Act II. Sc. I.

HELEN *and* SAFFISE

coming from an inner room, whose door is visible. HELEN
has her hat and shawl on.

Hel. Now I have seen those muslins, which I think,
　　Saffise, will well become you, I must go.
　　　Remember! I shall help you make them up?
Saff. No. When you have so much to do, indeed!
Hel. Yes, but then what I do is all for pay.
　　And I should like, so much, to do some work
　　To help a friend, or merely for her love:
　　My fingers would fly twice as fast.
　　　　　　　　　　　　Saff. I 'll see.
　　But why, dear, do you hurry so? your brother
　　Will call for you, you know.
　　　　　　　　　　　Hel. But not so soon.
　　I am not well [*sighing.*]; and but that I am so,
　　My father never would have let me come:
　　He thought 't would do me good. 'T is almost dark.
　　Good-bye, Saffise. Ah! there is brother now!
　　　　　　　　　[*delighted, and moving as if to go.*
　　No, there are two. [*recoiling.*

Enter, MANFRED *and* OSCAR.

MANFRED *and* HELEN *gaze at one another in mute amaze-*
ment, which in MANFRED *immediately changes*
to a look of dismay and sorrow, while
HELEN *drops her eyes.*

Osc. [*pulling Manf. aside.*

What say you now? [*Going to Saff.*] Saffise.
ᶦ *He touches* SAFFISE *on the shoulder as he passes*
her and beckons to her to follow him to the inner room.
She remonstrates with him in dumb-show. He gesticulates
violently, but without noise, in return, and after some
further resistance, he pushing her by the arm,
and whispering, she reluctantly follows,
bending her eyes on MANFRED *as*
she withdraws.

The door closes without noise on OSCAR *and* SAFFISE.

Manf. Miss Mattison —— [*gravely.*

Hel. [*who, from her position as well*
as emotion, is not aware of the
retreat of Saffise.

Sir! — I am going ——

Manf. Stay!

Helen, —[*laying his hand on her arm. She trembles,*
and stands as if incapable of motion, but
with her face still turned to the wings
of the scene as in the act of going out.

sadly.] Why are you here?

[*She looks up with surprise.*

Is this — Saffise —

Is she your friend?

    Hel. O yes; I like her much.

Manf. [*in turn surprised.*

  What a strange answer! [*looks at her inquiringly.*

    Do you visit her —

Here — often — in this house?

    Hel. Not very often.

This is the second time that I am here.

I must go now — 't is getting dark. Saffise. [*turning*

      round. She starts.

Where is she gone? And sir, — your brother ——

      [*in great alarm.*

She looks at MANFRED *once, earnestly, who has his eyes bent*
on her, his arms folded, then rushes to go out.

    MANFRED *intercepts her.*

      Manf. Stop.

Answer me but one question ere you go.

What brought you to this place, my child?

     Hel. This place?

    [*looking around her with increasing*
     terror, at which Manfred takes her
     hand, his expression losing its
     harshness.

It is Saffise's room. She had me come

To look at dresses she is making up.

Manf. [*eagerly.*] Ah! Did she go for you — this girl?

     Hel. She did.

    [*looking at him with fresh surprise.*

I was not well [*confused.*], and did not wish to come.

Manf. Why did you then?

              Hel. How could I, sir, refuse

Such a slight favor! and my father thought

My spirits would be better if I came.

Was it then wrong? and may I now go home?

Manf. [*clasping her hand, and gazing admiringly in her*
               face, at which she shrinks.

Go home? and wrong? you innocent child! go home?

Yes, and I will go with you; and you shall,

Before I leave you, promise, Helen dear,

Never to see again this wicked girl.

Do not so tremble! What have you to fear?

Do you not see that I am with you now,

I, Manfred Ferguson, and none beside? [*she trembles*
               and looks round.

What then shall harm you?

              Hel. O sir, let me go.

Do not retain my hand! and do not speak,

O do not, sir [*bursting into tears.*] in such a voice to me!

I am very weak, you see, my nerves are shook,

And though it shames me much, I needs must weep.

Manf. God help you, Helen! and God help me too!

For I am weak as you; and here — alone! ——

       [*gazing at her passionately, and folding her*
         hands in both of his.

Hel. [*endeavoring to extricate herself.*

    Sir — let us go, at once! — for Heaven's sake!

For your sweet cousin's sake! do let me go!

Manf. My cousin's!   Yes, yes, come! to stay
    Would make me, what I never yet have been,
    And shame to speak — a liar of me!   Come.
    Are you wrapt warm? [*timidly endeavoring to adjust*
                                her shawl.   She trembles.
                    this shawl is very thin.
But yet, the night-air is not chill.   And were it,
'T were better face it than stay here.   Come, come!
            [*He draws her arm through his, and Exeunt.*

                    Enter
Oscar, *bursting from the inner room, followed coolly by*
    Saffise, *who shrugs her shoulders.*

Osc. Curse on your house!
                Saff. Your folly, man, curse that!
    Did I not want to stay?
                Osc. I' faith, you did!
    You hop'd to catch my brother in your nets.
Saff. No matter what I hop'd, sir.   Had we staid,
    Would those nice questions have been put, d' you think,
    Or the girl answer'd?
                Osc. How could I foresee
    The milk-and-water fool would parley thus? —
    The patriarch Joseph was a rake to him!
Saff. Goodness! d' you read the Bible?
                    Osc. Do you dare
    To pass your jokes on me at such a time?
    Now, when my plans are all blown to the devil?
Saff. I don't see that.   You ruin'd me in the street, —

Met me there first, and then we met again,
And from the street came houses, — and then came
Saffise to be ——
       Osc. What Manfred may make Helen.
I 'll follow the game, and see what comes of it.
                     [Exit, impetuously.

Saff. And may you break your neck in the pursuit!
If scoundrels, like yourself, alone be men,
We women had better marry our own kind,
And save us from the sin of stocking Hell.
Ah! I 'd go there ten years before my time
For one kiss from your "milk-and-water fool"!
        She moves to the inner-room door, and
                Scene closes.

SCENE III.

*A public square, with streets opening into it.   It is nightfall,
and the lamps are lighted. —   Enter, from one of the
streets on the left wing, and furthest in the depth of the
stage,* MANFRED *and* HELEN.   *As they come forward to
the centre of the square,* OSCAR *is seen to issue from the
same street, wrapped closely in his cloak, with the collar
drawn round his cheeks.   He skulks into the angle of the
steps of one of the houses on the left, and remains there
covered by its shadow.*

Hel.   Pray, do not, do not further with me go?
Yonder 's the street I live in [*pointing to her right.*
                                          and not far.
It is not right that you should see me home.
My brother too will seek me.   Should you meet! —
                                          [*with alarm.*
O me! it is a dreadful thing, to feel
So guilty!
        Manf. Guilty, Helen? you!   And why?
Hel.   I know not, — but I feel it must be wrong,
To be with you — I should feel so asham'd
To have the eyes that love me see me now.
O sir, pray let me go!   I — sir —— Good night·
God bless you for your kindness! and — good night.
                                          [*Going.*
Manf. Helen, [*she stops directly.*] — dear Helen! [*taking
                                          her hand.*

I — It is so hard
To part thus and — forever. [*Helen bursts into tears.*
Do not cry!

Hel. O sir, forgive me; it is very childish:
It seems to me I have done nothing else
But cry, by the hour, ever since ——

Manf. I durst,
Weak, wicked that I was, avow my love.
There, now the word is said, that never again,
Never can be recall'd, — though thus to say it,
To you, you innocent child, is deadly wrong, —
Helen! — dear Helen! — Helen of my soul!
*He already holds her hand
in his left hand, and at these expressions of endearment,
each of which is tenderer in tone than the one that precedes it,
he passes his right arm round her waist,
and presses her to him.*
Say, if you must now leave me — and you must,
'T is terrible risk to your pure fame to stay —
Say you will come again.

Hel. O no, no!

Manf. No?
Do you not love me then? [*mournfully.*
Hush! do not sob;
Think, we are standing in the public street,
Helen, [*with deep tenderness.*
I know you love me. [*His head drops over
hers, and their faces seem to touch.*
Helen! [*murmuring.*]

kissing her passionately.] love!
For a moment,
both seem overcome: then MANFRED *continues, with ardor,*
but still in a low voice.

    Our breaths have mingled, and our souls are one:
No more you will refuse me; now to part,
After so brief a moment of delight,
Would be to kill us both with vain regret.
You will come back to me?

Hel. [*mournfully, yet with much tenderness.*

                          Alas! for what?
Since parting is such pain — and oh, I own
That it is very bitter — why again? ——

Manf. Would I renew it? Oh, because! —— Ask not!
I know but that I have you with me now:
To part with you forever —— Helen, speak!
Could *you* endure it, and your heart not break?

Hel. Where then? and when? [*in a low, agitated voice.*
                    Manf. Here, where we are,
The moment you can come to me.
                      Hel. O me!
My father! [*in a tone of deep anguish.*
              Never from his good, fond heart,
Have I hid anything. Do not ask me! pray,
Do not! indeed, indeed, I dare not! I
Should die of grief, to look on his white head,
And feel in my heart I 'd done him such a wrong
O it is better in my lonely bed to weep
For not having done it, than to weep it done!

Manf. You are an angel! Yes, it is a sin
To have concealments from the heart that trusts us,
And trusts us for it thinks that we have none:
And from a parent, folly it is as sin.
Helen, I cannot lie —— Yet, oh my God!
Have mercy! it is but for once — but once!

Hel. O no, no, do not tempt me! do not! Sir —
I — I am going — God — God bless you ever!
> [*endeavoring to leave him.*
> *Manf.* Ah!

You do not love me then?
> *Hel.* O, I will come!

I will! do not say that! [*putting her hands into his*
> *with great eagerness.*
> *Manf.* Heaven bless you now! [*He*
> *kisses her again, folding her in his embrace.*

But, can you escape without its being known?

Hel. I shall go up to my room —— [*bursting into tears.*
> *Manf.* Hush! do not cry.

Hel. I cry to think of my father — nothing more.

Manf. Fear not; he will not know it. — The house-door?
Will not the noise betray you?
> *Hel.* At that hour

It never is bolted; the room-doors are all clos'd.
Yet, should they open, should my brother come
Out in the passage, ere I pass the door! —
It is a fearful risk. [*shuddering.*
> *Manf.* Do not think so. [*pressing her sooth-*
> *ingly to him.*

Your soft light step, their dreaming not of this,
The wintry night, and the dark hall —— Is 't dark?
Hel. Yes, there is no light burning there; we are poor.
Manf. Hush, darling! It is Manfred that you speak to.
Hel. And oh, it is for that, I should not come!
Manf. Hush, hush again! [*kissing her.*

     When will this be? what hour?

Hel. The soonest I can take. Be near the door
Within an hour, say, from now. But oh,
You never will ask this of me again?
Promise it, or I come not!

    Manf. By my soul —
By honor, by my God, and by — our love! [*again
         kissing her.*

Hel. And you will not detain me long?

      Manf. No, no; even now
I hurry you off: go, Helen; or no, come! [*putting her
         arm under his.*

Hel. But at the head of the street, we part.

       Manf. And then,
I follow you till I see you in your home.

Hel. But not too near. Ah see! see what a thing
It is to be so guilty!

    Manf. Helen, peace! [*softly.*
The guilt is mine; for you are innocent still,
And yield to this deception for my sake —
For my love, Helen, is it not?

    [*embracing and kissing her again.*
      Ah yes!

Never shall you repent it. And now come.

They move diagonally
across the scene, arm in arm ; and OSCAR,
at the moment, comes out from his hiding-place, and follows
them cautiously, yet near enough to hear
the final words.

In less than an hour from now, remember, sweet,
Manfred will wait you.

They part at the corner,
or wing of the scene, in the remotest part of the stage,
OSCAR *again receding into the shadow, though now on the*
right hand, until HELEN *disappears, and,*
after a moment, MANFRED *follows, when*
OSCAR *comes forward again.*

     Osc. Like a dog, in the street.
I thought the pretty scene would never have done.
Pest on the fellow ! And I must wait still,
To know where this rare meeting is to be,
And when ; for nothing could I hear but this :
"Manfred will wait you." How egregious fine !
Could not the gentleman have said, *I 'll* wait ?
So much for having a fine name ! Now, had
Our father — but perhaps it was our dam
Was so romantic in her tastes — but chosen
To call you *Tom,* I think you had been more plain.
Thomas will wait you, would have sounded rare !
Pomposity ! — But who the devil is this ?

He has been moving back again to
the left, and now, with his back to the
audience, is about encountering RICHARD
MATTISON, *who is seen coming from the street at*
which MANFRED *and* HELEN, *and finally himself had*
appeared. At this moment, VINCENT, *muffled in a Span-*
ish cloak, but with his face uncovered, issues from the same
side of the scene, — but close to the proscenium, as OSCAR
and RICHARD *are farthest in the background.* VIN-
CENT *is about to pass in front, as* OSCAR *speaks*
in a loud tone.

Oh, Mattison, it 's you, is 't!

VINCENT *starts at the name, looks at them a moment, then*
eagerly muffling his face with the cloak, moves over the
stage, toward the quarter where MANFRED *and*
HELEN *have disappeared, passing directly in*
front, the whole breadth of the scene, then
turning straight up on the right, but
very slowly, and eying from time
to time the party, over the
muffle of his cloak.

       You 're too soon.

Rich. I know it, but I come now from a place
Where I had look'd to find my sister.   But,
Your brother, sir, it seems, was earlier there.

Osc.   True.

  Rich. How?   You knew it?   ·

       Osc. Only now, i' faith.

He saw her home, and, with her on his arm,

·Pass'd ·- half an hour ago.

                Rich. Good night.

                        Osc. Eh, stop!

Did you not hear me? half an hour ago.

Your sister is by this time snug at home.

Rich. I know not that. [*still endeavoring to go.*

                Osc. But I do; for my brother

I left just now at the house. So, you will see,

You will not find him as you think. Now go,

And wait me at the place you know of. Go;

I 'll follow you in a minute.

                Rich. Why not now?

Osc. O, I 've a fancy of my own detains me. [*signifi-*

                                cantly.

It shall not be for long. A word, a kiss,

The little flutterer 's soon put off, you know,

And a new night will serve her turn as well.

There go.

       Rich. Ah, ah! yon are a sad rake!

                    Osc. I!

'Faith, if I be, my teeth are open, though.

Rich. Yes, and for that I like you: not as ——

                      Osc. Go!

                    [*pushing him off.*

I am busy now, I tell you. And besides,

Tease me, and, sir, I will not come at all;

And that would be your loss, — for, hark! I have

    news.

Rich. What! of the villain's ——

Osc. Of my brother, sir.
You 'll please remember that, and be less rude.
I.league with you in pity of your sister,
In charity for yourself, and for your sire :
No further.

      Rich. Pardon me.

          Osc. There go.

OSCAR *turns his back, as if his purpose were to pursue the way
he was taking when they met, and* RICHARD *turns off at
the right wing, close to the proscenium.* VINCENT
*immediately follows, and disappears in the same
direction, before* OSCAR *again returns.*

              Another
Of the predestinate asses!   A mere boy,.
That thinks my roughness openness : to him !
Open to him ! [*with an expression of the most intense
contempt.*] But, 'faith, he was well off,
For here comes Manfred now.

        [*looking toward the quarter where Manf. had
made his exit with Helen.*

             Had they but met,
Simplicity again had o'ermatch'd cunning:
These candid people soon make darkness light.

       Re-enter MANFRED.

What, Manfred! you?   Where have you left the girl ?
You just miss'd falling foul of her own brother.
How pale you are!   What ails you?   Why not speak !
Manf. [*grasping his hand and speaking solemnly.*

I have seen a sight——

     Osc. The devil you have! A ghost?

Manf. Don't mock me, Oscar; 't is no time for jest.

Had you but seen—— I 'll tell you: listen. When

I had left that innocent girl—— But, by the by,

You must admit you did traduce her vilely.

Saffise was not——

     Osc. In that point, I admit

I was deceiv'd. Go on now. When you left——

Manf. Poor Helen at her home, the parlor-light

Shone through a half-clos'd shutter. The desire

To see her face once more, to see her too

When unaware a lover's eye was watching,

And in her family-circle unrestrain'd,

Seem'd nowise wrong, nor its indulgence mean.

I stoop'd to the crevice. By a table sat

A reverend man, of mien more apostolic

Than ever painter drew. A length of hair,

Glistening and white as silver, downward floated

In waves to his very shoulders; and his brow,

*Whether the book he read from so inspir'd,

Or 't was the habitual feeling of his soul,

His brow, and the sweet outline of his lips,

Spoke of true nobleness, candor without guile.

O brother, when I saw this sight, my heart

Reproach'd me for its weakness, and Remorse

Seem'd to have blanch'd those locks for only me.

What then, when suddenly the parlor-door

Flew open, and poor Helen, rushing in,

Threw her arms round the old man's neck, and wept!

Osc.   You saw it?

     Manf. Yes; he rais'd her head, the light
Glanc'd on her tears. — Then words were interchang'd,
And Helen heavily sigh'd. —

           ·   *Osc.* You heard her?

                      Manf. No;
Her bosom visibly heav'd.   The old man then
Laid his hand gently on her head, and parting
The beautiful hair upon her forehead, kiss'd it.
She took a lamp — her hand so shook, poor girl,
She could not light it, and the old man help'd her —
And to the door went Helen, tearful. —

                Osc. Ah! [*affecting
            a sigh of relief from fatigue.*
The air is chilly.

      Manf. Is it? [*abstractedly.*] — But behold!
With sudden impulse coming back, she fell
At the old man's feet upon her knees, her face
Hid in her hands, which folded on his lap.
She seem'd to ask his blessing; for, uplifting
His tremulous hands and glistening eyes to Heaven,
He said aloud — I heard him through the pane —
⁊"Bless her, thou God of justice! bless my child!
And on her innocent spirit let not sin
Drop its decaying mildew! from her brow
Let Care remove its shadow, and her eyes
Sparkle once more with happy light; for Thou,
Thou knowest, my God, how very pure she is,

How true her life has been to Thee and me!
On her sad pillow, let Thy angels' wings
This night shed slumber, fanning to repose
Her troubled spirit, and her shatter'd nerves —
Too weak for their sore trial — making whole !
So shall her heart have strength to bear its load.
Help, God our Father! help my child!   Amen!"

Osc. Excellent poetry ! And the result?

Manf. Are you so cruel? — Hear then the result.
That *Silver Head* has sav'd both her and me.
This night I am to meet her. Should she come! —
Those white locks shall be round her like a veil,
Nor shall my passion lift it.

     Osc. What means that?
Where were you then to meet her ? at what time ?

Manf Within an hour, here, in the public street.

Osc. Choice place! What purpose would such folly serve ?

Manf. To make me madder ! for a moment fill,
To leave it emptier than before, that void,
Which in my heart keeps aching ever, ever,
With a sick pang, when Helen is away ;
A pang, I fancy, he who knows not, Oscar,
Never has ——

   Osc. Been a man of blood and brains.
'T is the old story: sensual sensation,
A gnawing natural as the lust to dine.
You are not made to starve, and will fare well.
But next time, Manfred, when you spread your table,
Let it not be, as now, *al fresco.*

Manf.. Peace!

You speak of Helen; and you speak to me.

I am not Oscar; nor is she Saffise.

Osc. No, but you both are human. Else, why meet?

Manf. Because I ask'd her. Haply, had we met,

Unheard that voice, those silver hairs unseen,

Conscience and Reason might have wept it. Now,

We part at once, or — never shall part more.

Osc. When was your blood made water? I've forgotten.

Manf. Ah! Hear me then. I swear it — by high Heaven!

You know my faith, how sacred : had I sworn

To kill her, I had stabb'd her with this hand. —

Now sleep in peace, thou venerable man!

No dust shall soil those silver locks for me,

Nor Helen's young heart break with grief of sin!

> [*Exit, at the left of the scene, nearest the*
> *proscenium — the quarter whence Vincent*
> *had entered. Oscar regards him with*
> *supreme contempt till he disappears.*

Osc. "Now sleep in peace, thou venerable man!" —

What a fine thing to have poetic brains! —

"Helen's young heart!" — You are not Oscar? [*with*
> *a tone of deep malignity.*] No;

Nor am I Manfred. Go! For all that 's said,

I'll ruin you both, despite the SILVER HEAD.

> [*Exit, at the right, where Richard had disap-*
> *peared, and the*

> *Drop falls.*

AOT THE FOURTH

SOENE I. *Sybil's boudoir, as in Act I., Sc. II.*

SYBIL.

She appears to have just entered.

Syb. [*looking pensively at the broken flowers which still
strew the floor.*

    Emblems indeed! How soon these scented leaves,
                  [*lifting one of them.*
    * Whose delicate freshness shrivels at my touch,
    Will lie so wither'd, never heat nor cold,
    Nor moisture, sensibly will affect them more!
    Yet for a while their perfume still survives —
    Their unseen virtue. Even so, poor Helen,
    Thy sensitive heart, that quivers at the touch
    Of its new passion, thrown thus under foot,
    Will take like changes. Yet, a just God grant
    Its precious fragrance may not quit the flower,
    While yet a leaf remains! — Strange, partial world!
    Plac'd but as I, had Helen been — how blest!
    And yet * — perhaps her lowly state, contrasted
    With her so delicate air, and artless grace,
    And her exceeding guilelessness of soul,
    Makes irresistible what else might fail.

'T is this scope of a power, for him and her
So dangerous, renders Helen's fate so hard.
And I, unfortunate, who drew her hither,
Meaning but good, yet doing fatal harm!

> [*Sinks into abstraction, gazing on the
> scattered flower-leaves.*

Enter MANFRED.

Manf. [*Smiling sadly.*
 What, cousin, musing on your misus'd gift!
Syb. Musing to moralize.
        Manf On Helen's fate,
Even as you said before. — I might so too. [*taking
                        up some of the leaves.*
Broken unwittingly, broken by a hand
That lov'd in other times to use you well,
Flowers, in whose fragile forms the spirit of beauty
Made rapturous worship for the impassion'd heart,
Nor God dissented, — broken by my hand,
Who can unite your scatter'd leaves again?

> [*He drops the petals, and clasps his hands earnestly.*
O! 't was an oath well sworn!
                Syb. What was? and when?
Manf. Ah, Sybil! I have seen — have that to tell! ——
Hush? 't is our uncle; we must be alone.

Enter SIR HENRY.

Sir H. At last, my dear boy! And where have you been?
It was not well, nor was it done like Manfred,

To leave without excuse your friend alone, —
Oscar too gone. But what is rather odd,
Vincent, the moment he is given to know
Yourself and Oscar have gone out together,
Mutters his own excuses, and is off!
Manf. Indeed! He fears to trust me; [*to himself.*
                                    and has cause.
Sir H. Are you so slippery? And, in truth, I see,
Now I look at you, all is not quite well.
But I am nowise curious,—nor need be:
With such a Mentor, though his beard 's still brown,
My good Telemachus cannot travel wrong,
Even where such Circes intercept his way. [*twining*
            his fingers affectionately in one of Sybil's curls.
Syb. Strange compliment! Good uncle, you are dull
As Manfred's Mentor at a flattering speech.
Oh that I had the enchantress' cup awhile,
To put a bristling hide on both your backs!
Sir H. 'T would be no new reqnital for the pains
Men take to please, to steal away their minds;
Would it be, Manfred?
            Manf. [*vacantly — starting from a fit of deep*
                abstraction.
                        Sir?
            Sir H. [*shaking his head knowingly at Sybil.*
                'T is done already.
Come, you will make a poor Ulysses' heir;
You play Elvino better; Circe here
Shall change to sweet Amina. I am come,

In fact to lead you to the music-room:
Uncle must have his favorite *Scene* again, —
Tutto è sciolto!

      Manf. Pray excuse me, sir.
Sybil will take some other part, alone.
To sing well sadly, one's heart must be gay.
To bid, in song, adieu for evermore
To consolation and the light of love,
Would not be easy, cousin, for me now.

                    [looking appealingly to Sybil.

Syb. Not if the song and truth must needs be one.
But then, Rubini never had grown fat.

    MANFRED *presses the ends of her fingers; and they*
             go out thus, hand in hand.

Sir. H. [*loitering.*

    Ah! this looks well! I shall be blest at last,
And Sybil's heirs will bear her uncle's name.
And such an offspring! 'T will outshine the stars.

                    [Exit, after them.

SCENE II.

A room in a tavern.
A lighted lamp suspended from the ceiling.

RICHARD MATTISON *is seen standing with his hat on and*
back to the fireplace, his hands in the pockets of his over-
coat: VINCENT *walking up and down with his arms*
folded, his cloak and hat still on. — VINCENT *is at the*
furthest end of the room, and with his back to the audi-
ence, as

Enter, OSCAR.

Osc. [*throwing back his cloak and taking off his hat, both*
of which he tosses on a table which is standing
in the middle of the room.
You see I have not kept you waiting long:
And now, to work. [*As he faces about, sees Vincent.*
What 's this? Whom have you here?

VINCENT *turns and looks at him steadily,*
his arms still folded.
Vincent!
Rich. The gentleman profess'd to have
Some business with you too, and would come in.

As RICHARD *speaks,* VINCENT *throws off*
his cloak deliberately, and lays it and his hat
on the table where OSCAR'S *are:* RICHARD *still standing,*
with his hat and overcoat on, without
shifting his position.

Osc. Fool! 't is my brother's friend and prompter!

Rich. A scoundrel's friend, and prompter for the Devil!

Vin. Indeed? [*making directly toward him with a deter-*
mined air : Rich., with equal resolution, but
with more violence, rushing to meet him.
Oscar steps between them.

Osc. Stop! both of you: this quarrel 's mine.
First, sir, for you, [*turning severely to Rich.*
let me not have again
To bid you, when my brother is your theme,
To characterize him by some milder name.
And now, sir, [*to Vinc. with a malignant smile.*
what occasion brings you here?
To gloss for me the " *truth without a flaw ?*"

Vin. To find its illustration, rather say;
To penetrate the schemes, and make them null,
Of a false friend and brother, and reopen
The eyes of this rash boy [*indicating Rich. by a slight*
motion of the head.
your arts have clos'd.

Osc. [*putting coolly back, with the palm of his hand, Rich-*
ard, who, at these words, is rushing upon Vincent.
And did your wisdom calculate the risk
Of this ambition to enact the spy,
Or think what heavy premium must be paid
For insight into schemes, which — say they be —
Can not concern you anywise at all?

Vin. For *spying*, sir, my open dealing now
Makes that sneer harmless: had I been dispos'd,

I might have gain'd my object ere you came,
And spar'd this person [*looking at Rich.*
                   cause for deep regret.
For risk, who knows me well as you, should know,
What Theodore Vincent's plain sense may advise
For Manfred's good, that does he as the friend
Of Manfred, and at once, nor counts the risk.

Osc. That we shall see. [*with a meaning smile.*
                   Here, Mattison, go up
To the billiardroom above us, draw aside
The keeper of 't, who happily keeps too
A shooting-gallery; give him this gold piece,
Mention my name, and bid him give you straight
His two best weapons, with a flask and balls,
And keep his tongue about it.

Rich. [*with astonishment and some degree of alarm.*
                   Do you mean it?

Osc. Look at us both; [*glancing round to Vincent.*
                   then ask me, if you can,
If I be serious. Go. [*Exit Richard.*
         Vin. And what by this
Does Mr. Oscar Ferguson propose?

Osc. To do that now, which I had meant to-morrow
To do in a colder field. Our fingers here
Will be more flexible, although the light [*looking care-
                   lessly up at the lamp.*
Is not, i' faith, so brilliant as the sun.

Vin. [*sternly.*] Sir, do you think, because yourself are mad,
That I am too?

Osc. Oh no, I am aware
That Mr. Vincent's wisdom, or "plain sense,"
Knows well the difference betwixt giving insult
And making reparation for it.
                              Vin. Ah! —
But no! you shall not force me into crime,
Nor to such folly as would make me lose
Both the world's reverence and your brother's love.
I have enough of courage to dare leave.   [*laying his
          hand on his cloak to lift it from the table.*
Osc. [*putting his own hand on the same.*
        You came, sir, uninvited, and you go
Without obtaining what in hopes to gain
You scrupled not to lay good manners by.
But I am hospitable, and entreat, insist,
That you will deign to make yourself at home.
Wait Mattison's return, and put him all
Such questions as you like; when that is done,
In honor of your struggle with good-breeding,
And freedom won from tyranny of shame,
We will together fire a *feu-de-joie.*
*Suddenly changing his manner to a perfect seriousness, with-
        out rudeness or impertinence.*
Sir, Mr. Vincent, men report you wise,
And honorable, and brave, and that all this
You are, and more, does Manfred love to think.
I will now put those qualities to proof.
This day I have borne gross insults from you twice;
First, in my brother's presence. —

Vin. [coldly and calmly.] 'T was provok'd.

Osc. Be it so; still an insult. And now here,
Before a fellow neither of us knows.
You are no bigot, sir, I will presume,
And, giving, in the fashion of the world,
Mortal offence, will not deny you are bound
To give such satisfaction for the affront
As 't is the fashion of the world to claim?

Vin. I do not.

Osc. [eagerly.] Then, to-morrow you had met,
As a brave man and honorable should,
The challenge I was fully bent to send?

Vin. As a brave man and honorable should,
Who has no fear to do the thing that 's right,
Refus'd to fight the brother of my friend.

Osc. My brother well might pity, but not love
A coward.

   Vin. Sir! — Enough. I 'll meet you.

      Osc. [joyfully.] Good.
To a brave man all times are equal: now
Will serve as well as to-morrow.

Enter RICHARD,

bearing the weapons, inclosed in the usual case.

    To Richard.] Set them down.

Vin. [indignantly.] No sir, now will not serve. I am no
  brawler
To fight in a tavern-room, no seconds by.

If you have no regard to name, I have.

To-morrow I will meet you, where you will.

Osc.   And that is, nowhere.   Go.   Be off!   I thought

To fight with a man: but you are none.   There, go.

> [*flinging his cloak to Vincent, insultingly, so*
> *that it strikes him heavily on the shoulder*
> *and in the face.*

Vin. [*sternly to Richard.*

Sir, bolt the door. [*To Oscar.*] I am ready.

> [*and he lays down the cloak. — Again*
> *to Richard, but mildly.*
>
> I know not

Aught of you, Mr. Mattison, nor why

You are present here, save what I can conjecture,

And too well, from your name.   Quite unprovok'd,

You have insulted me most grossly; this

I do forgive you ——

> *Rich.*   Sir — [*impatiently.*
>
> *Vin.* Be not impatient;

What I have yet to say is briefly this:

If I should fall in this disgraceful conflict,

I charge you, as a man, to tell the world,

That Theodore Vincent, with his latest breath,

Protested against such a fight, and yielded

Only at last to shun a worse disgrace.

Osc. [*opening the case, and taking out the weapons as he*
     speaks.

And should I fall, see that you hawk about

My dying-confession and last speech as this:

That Oscar Ferguson would shoot his foe
Wherever he found him, but, being shot himself,
Felt quite as well content his blood should soak
A carpet as bedabble a green field. [*takes out the flask*
and balls.

Rich. [*apparently horror-struck.*
 Gentlemen! this is horrid! must not be! —
Sir [*to Vin.*] — Mr. Ferguson [*to Osc.*] —
 Osc. [*taking out the caps from the bottom of the*
 powder-flask, and examining them.
 Will you hold your tongue?
Else, leave the room, and let us fight alone.
Rich. [*angrily.*] I 'd have you, Mr. Ferguson, remember,
 In ordering me, that I am not your slave.
I shall remain, for Mr. Vincent's sake,
As much as for your own.   But pray, be civil.
Osc. [*carelessly, and, as before, without turning his head.*
 Pardon.—— [*To Vin.*] You load for me, and I for you.
Which weapon will you take?   They seem alike.
 [*looking at them, as he holds them, with the*
 air of a connoisseur, then handing them
 both to Vin.
Vin. This, which is next me, then. [*taking it.*
 . *Osc.* The one that 's left
I charge for you. [*handing Vin. the powder-flask.*
 But now, that I reflect,
Had we not better go above? the noise
Will cause no wonder in the gallery.
 Vin. No;

If 't must be thus, it may as well be here: [*charging
his weapon.*

To light the shooting-room would cost us time.

Osc.   And others than yourself have none to spare.

[*looking first at his watch, and then
significantly to Rich.*

Make haste.   The ball and mallet, sir. [*handing them,
and taking in turn the flask.*

But, stay:

Above, the shots may be repeated; here,

At the first sound, the house may be upon us.

We had better, sir, adjourn.

              Vin. Perhaps adjourn

For good.   Proceed; or you will make me think

You want your brother's courage, as his honor.

Osc.   Ah! I deserv'd that; 't is a fair return. [*ramming
home his charge.*

The mallet? have you done? [*Vin. hands it.*

              One shot may do.

                [*forcing in the ball.*

But who the devil is there? [*the door violently shook
from within.*

            The cap, sir, quick.

[*handing it to Vin., and fitting one on his own weapon.*

Don't mind it, Mattison. [*the door shaken still more
violently.*

           Are you ready, sir? [*To Vin.*

          — *They exchange weapons.*

Choose your own corner.

*Vincent rapidly places himself at the left angle,
while Oscar takes as quickly the corner diagonally opposite,
and which is close to the door that is still shaking
from the efforts made within.*

We have just the space.
One, two, three, fire. Quick; call, sir. [*to Rich.* —
The door is burst open, and, rushing in,

Enter Meddleham.

Medd. No you don't!
Coming against Oscar, *the impetus given
him by the resistance of the door throws down the former,
whose pistol explodes.*
You 're in a hurry, my fine fellow.
Osc. [*rising, and striking passionately with
the weapon at Medd., who avoids the
blow, which sends Oscar stagger-
ing past him.*
Fool!
Take that for interfering.   Mattison,
Why do you rush between us? knock him down,
Or tumble him from the room.   Curse on you, sir!
Will you go out? [*endeavoring to turn Medd. out.*
Medd. [*struggling to disengage himself.*
What name was that you said?
Mattison? [*in a tone of surprise.*
Vin. [*who has laid down his weapon and put on
his cloak.*
Mr. Ferguson, good night.

The play is ended here: you may renew it,
Even when you please; but on a fitter stage.

> [*Exit, hat in hand, — while Richard hastily re-*
> *stores the implements to the case, and hurries*
> *out with it. Oscar lets go of Meddleham,*
> *who seems to take the affair in perfect*
> *good part, while Oscar gazes on him*
> *with both rage and surprise.*

Medd. Ferguson too! Why what the deuse is this?
Which one is Ferguson? Are you, sir, he?

Osc. (An odd fish this!) I am, sir, at your pleasure.

> [*bowing sarcastically.*

Is it to kick you from the room at once,
Or first to beat you handsomely, to teach you
A meddler gets less thanks than broken bones?

Medd. You have not hit it quite, sir, there: my name
Is Meddleham, not Meddler; 't is so spell'd,
That is to say; but people choose to call it,
And so my grandsire did among the rest,
Middleum. As for broken bones, young man,
Perhaps Ralph Meddleham gives as well as takes.

Osc. Will you then give me, sir, the satisfaction
To see Ralph take himself out of this room.
I pay for it, and want no meddlers here,
Whether their hams be Middle hams or Meddles.

Medd. That 's right enough, although 't is wrongly said.
But first, my young impertinent, will 't please you
Who are so ready with your fist and pistol,
Or boast to be, to tell me if you be

One of the nephews of Sir Henry here,
Old Colonel Ferguson?
   Osc. [*surprised.*] What 's that to you?
Medd. More than you think, and much to you besides.
You are not Manfred, surely?
        Osc. What comes next?
           [*to himself.*
Truly, I am. [*after looking for a moment narrowly at*
  Medd.] What then?
      Medd. Why then this world
Is still more given to lying than I had thought it.
             [*Exit.*
Osc. [*solus.*] Then has your charity outweigh'd your
  brains. —
  Meddleham — Middleum — Ralph — Who can this be?
           [*thoughtfully.*
Yet, now I think, the name resembles one
That when a child I heard my mother mention.
Whatever though the intruder has to do
With me or Manfred, this I thank him for,
For bursting-in that door ere quite too late;
For, whether I had shot Vincent, or he me,
My schemes to-night had equally fallen through.
I must command this temper. But what keeps
That would-be man, Miss Nelly's saucy brother,
So long away? [*looking at his watch.*] A genteel
  second that!
It had read well in the prints, a petty clerk,
Of some small warehouseman, sole witness 'tween

The fashionable Vincent and myself! —
How well though Vincent bore himself! 'T is strange:
My hate for him was mortal: since I find
The man has blood like other men, and nerve —
Devilish good nerve too! — should we never fight,
The disappointment will not make me thin.
But where 's this stripling! Heaven send, as yet,
He have not shot himself! My work once done,
He may as soon as he pleases, and so spare
Some better man the task of ridding him
Of brains he never uses. I must see.

> [*Goes to the door, and opens it, to listen. The
> Scene closes on him in the act.*

SCENE III.

Saffise's parlor — as in Act II., Sc. I.

SAFFISE, *alone,*
reclining on the couch. A plain lamp burning
on the table.

Saff. [springing up.
I'll do it! I will, I will, I will. The wretch
                              [comes forward.
Shall not make *me* his tool, to fling away
Like a broken chisel, when I've serv'd his turn;
Cursing me too while using me, because
He has no skill for his work. The bungling knave!
I'll cut his fingers for him, to the bone! —
Now let me see: if Helen has been weak
Like other girls, and Oscar's brother's blood
Is half as hot as it should be from his looks,
All 's over, and the Colonel's favor is lost.
The more fool he, to cut his darling off
For kissing a pale-fac'd girl without his leave!
A thing he has often done himself, I 'd swear,
And never ask'd his nephews how they lik'd it.
But Oscar shall gain nothing by the chance,
Except what he deserves, — a traitor's pay.
To expose him, it is true, will shame myself;
And so he thinks I will not. He shall find,
Saffise will be reveng'd at any cost!

Saffise, the "*slut*": I have not forgot the words.
My God, how should I! — "*that this gentle girl*
Should make a playmate of a slut like me !"
Ah! they shall cost him dear. I'll tell it all,
I will — on the instant — if the "gentle girl "

> [*with bitterness.*

Herself is standing by, and the poor slut
Is turn'd into the street with shame — I will!

> [*swaying herself on her toes, her figure rising*
> *and falling with every clause, as she ges-*
> *ticulates passionately. —— Walking up,*
> *toward the door of the inner room.*

They 'll not refuse to let me see Sir Henry.
Should *he* be there — the brother of my Turk! —

> [*takes up the lamp and goes before a mirror.*

How dull my eyes look! I could tear them out.
It is this lock of hair that has got misplac'd.

> [*endeavoring to arrange it.*

I 'll let it all out; it looks vilely, all.

Lets down the whole of her hair ; then gathers it together in
her hands, and begins to dress it in the manner
of her sex.

But everything seems wrong! [*letting it all down*
> *again.*

> This paltry shawl!

> [*taking it pettishly off*

One of my *master's* gifts — mean like himself.

> [*thrusts it from her with her foot.*

I 'll make my toilet over — hair and all.

Oh, that I were as Helen! [*coming down, in her dis-*
array.

Could I win
But one of those sweet words he spoke to her,
But one look from his beautiful, thoughtful eyes,
One look that did not mock me like his brother's,
I 'd make of my hair a cloth to dust his shoes.
I would! I 'd be the vilest thing in the world,
So I might for an hour sit at his feet,
And hear him say, *Saffise, you are no slut!*
She sobs, and drawing her hair before her eyes, uses it to
staunch her tears; and the scene closes on her
thus standing.

SCENE IV.

The parlor at Mattison's, as in Act II., Sc. II.

MATTISON *and* MEDDLEHAM,
seated by a table lighted by a plain but shaded lamp.

Matt. Yes, that is very true; my father's sister
Marry'd a Meddleham.
Medd. Who was my father.
Matt. We are then cousins? [*extending his hand cordially*
to Medd.

Medd. [*taking it frankly and heartily.*] Happily, I trust,
  For both of us, when you know all. Enough
  For the time present, that, except your own,
  And one more family, of which anon,
  I am lonely in the world now, and am come
  A weary, weary way from the Far West,
  To lay my old bones with you, if you will.
  But tell me now, how many, cousin Mark,
  You have in family besides your son.
Matt. One only, but an angel upon earth,
  If ever were.
     Medd. A daughter then? And pretty?
Matt. Beautiful! as a star in a winter's night.
  But not more beautiful than good. O sir,
  Her graces and her virtues are the rose
  Blossoming in a wilderness to me,
  Making all garden and perpetual bloom.
Medd. Where is she? Sha' n't I see her?
        Matt. Not to-night:
  She came home from her daily work, poor child,
  Earlier than usual and exceeding sad,
  And is but now retired.
     Medd. Her daily work!
  You are poor then? [*with a kind of exultation, and*
       looking about him, on the furniture
       of the room, &c.
   Matt. [*gravely.*] We complain not. Are you glad?
Medd. Glad it is in my power to do you good;
  Glad —— You shall see to-morrow! And her name?

Matt. Helen.

   Medd. My mother's!

     Matt. Thence deriv'd.

       Medd. That 's well.

How I shall love her! [*rubbing his hands.*

    Would I were as sure

Of her fine brother; but the friends I see

The young man leag'd with do not promise much.

Matt. How! Mr. Meddleham!

      Medd. Bah! call me Ralph.

D' you think, man, that because I have liv'd away,

And never look'd upon your face before,

You are unknown to me? I have cherish'd long

A world of love, that now has grown so big

My bosom would not hold it: so I came

To vent it all upon its proper objects,

On you and yours, and other kin besides.

Why, cousin Mark, I knew your Helen's name

And Richard's long ago, and if I ask'd

Those questions of the girl, 't was but to sound

Your own affection, and to ascertain

If private rumor had reported well.

Besides, they tell me that I have a trick

Of questioning people where I should be dumb.

But if I had not, how should I be wise?

Matt. But my boy, Richard? He is rash, I know,

And very wilful, yet his morals still

Have seem'd correct: what were those friends you

  mean?

Medd. One Manfred Ferguson —

      Matt. What!   Heaven forbid!

          [in much alarm.

Medd. And so say I, although 't is rather late:

 For of all impudent fellows I ever met

 This Master Manfred will bear off the palm.

Matt. You dream! you are misled!   What Manfred 's

 this?

Medd. The Colonel's nephew, old Sir Henry's here

 The name is not so common, I should think.

Matt. Manfred!   Why he 's a hero of romance,

 A pattern of the rarest qualities

 Of head and heart a man can well possess.

 I said not " Heaven forbid!" because of that:

 I would to Heaven he were my Richard's friend!

Medd. Then you must want to bring your Richard up

 A duelist, or a champion of the ring:

 For, hark you, Mark, your " hero of romance "

 Offer'd to kick me, try'd to beat my brains out,

 And came near putting a bullet through my leg.

Matt. This is some strange mistake!   Explain it: where

 Was this?

  Medd. There 's no mistake at all, save what

 Those wise ones fell into, who taught me too

 This Manfred was a hero of romance —

 Such a romance as Tom Crib might have writ!

 Hear then.

    The time being heavy on my hands,

 I stroll'd this evening to the billiardroom

Of the hotel where I had just put up.   .
Presently comes a young man in great haste,
His features ruffled strangely, takes aside
The keeper of the room, slips in his hand
Some money, whispers, and they both go out.
Following in a little while, I see them
Descending, both, the stairs that led above,
The young man having in his hands a case
Of questionable shape.   They part; and then,
Coming more near, I hear the man observe,
"Remember! 't is no fault of mine, sir!"—"None,"
Answers the youth: "Say nothing, that is all!"
This youth was Richard Mattison, your son.
Matt. God help me!   What is coming?
                                    Medd. So said I, —
And watching stealthily the young man's course,
And following at a proper distance, came
To a room of the floor below he just had enter'd.
Almost immediately the door is lock'd.
"Aha!" thought I, "I see what you are after;
But I shall spoil your sport, my gentle doves!"
I listen'd long enough, and saw enough
Through the keyhole too, to make belief conviction,
And finally burst the door in, just in time
To save two fools from making one fool less.
Matt. Don't stop! [*eagerly, with an expression of anguish.*
        Medd. I did not; for my body, coming
Prone on the nearest fighter, knock'd him down.
The hair of his pistol being ready set, ...

Off goes the weapon, right betwixt my legs.
But, as if risk of maiming were n't enough,
My gentleman, rising, with his popgun's stock
Tries to beat out my brains!
    Matt. [*grasping his arm.*] 'T was not my son?
Medd. No, your son rush'd between us.
                        Matt. Ah! thank God!
And yet, he was the other combatant!
Medd. No, he was not: how can you be so silly?
He went for the weapons, that was all, and stood,
As second in common, by, to see fair play.
The other was a man more old than either,
And seem'd the decentest fellow of all three.
Matt. But sure you said, that one of them was Manfred?
Medd. I did; I had it from his very lips —
After he had offer'd, courteously, to beat me,
Or kick me out of the room, if I preferr'd.
Matt. Strange!
          Medd. True not less. But, to conclude the tale,
Hearing this Manfred call your son by name,
Politely bidding him knock the meddler down,
Or tumble me from the room, — romantic, that!
I follow'd the latter, met him coming back —
Learn'd your address, and straightway hasten'd
    hither, —
Chiefly because he told me I must not.
And now, what say you, cousin, to my tale?
Is this good company that Richard keeps?
Matt. I say still, there is some mistake. But wait:

My son must soon be home.

      Medd. When we shall see.

Meantime, this is dry talking, cousin Mark:

What have you got?

     Matt. I soon can give you tea.

Medd. Tea! 't is not hearty. But perhaps you are

One of good Matthew's people?

       Matt. No, I am temperate

Not by forswearing every mirthful drink,

Which were ascetic, but by using them

Only as I would have my boy use pleasure,

A little at a time, and "far between."

Medd. [*pressing his hand admiringly and affectionately.*

  Philosopher and poet, as they told me.

Let us then have some punch this winter evening,

And, if you have no spirit and lemons here,

We 'll send your woman for them. What 's her name?

   [*rising briskly, and ringing the parlor-bell.*

Kitty?

Matt. No, Molly. [*smiling.*

    Medd. Molly, is it? [*knocks on the floor with*

   his stick ; then, running like a boy to the door

   and opening it, cries out into the passage.

       Molly!

Put on the kettle, Molly, — not for tea!

MATTISON *watches him with a benevolent smile —*

   and the Drop falls.

ACT THE FIFTH.

SCENE I.　*The room of the tavern, as in Act IV., Sc. II.*

The lamp burning, as before.

OSCAR *and* RICHARD.

Rich. Wherefore not now? [*taking up his hat with an air
of restrained impatience.*
　Osc. Because it is too soon.
Have I not said, the high contracting parties
Agreed — and seal'd the treaty with their lips —
　　　　　[*Rich. restraining an impulse of anger.*
An hour and more should intervene, between
That last dear parting and the auspicious time
When the fair Helen, issuing from her chamber,
Should make a Meneläus of her 'pa,
And meet the Paris, Manfred, in the streets?
Rich. [*furiously.*
　Stop, sir! What does this language mean? to me?
Osc. [*shrugging his shoulders.*
　'Faith, I might answer you, my lad, in brief,
That you may let it mean even what you please.
But we 'll not have those pistols brought again;
They go off much too promptly: so, I say,

It is to curb your temper that I jest.

What should I gain insulting your chaste sister,

[Rich. winces again,.

Or jesting at your father's silver hairs?

I sacrifice my brother to spare both.

Rich. Well, well! But do not speak with such an air;

It seems to mock me, though you mean so well.

Osc. And now is the time to prove it. [looking at his watch.

But remember, [laying

his hand on Richard's sleeve.

.It is my brother, sir, you go to meet.

Though you arrest him in his wicked purpose,

You are to use no violence; no weapons

Must be employ'd that may endanger life.

And yet — Alas! he is stronger than a lion,

And quite as brave. 'T is dreadful — but I fear

I cannot hinder you. But be humane;

It is the law of God as well as man.

Rich. I will defend my honor at all costs.

Let me go, Mr. Ferguson! [bursting from him. Exit.

Osc. [after a moment's pause of great agitation.

No, no! [to himself. —

Calling aloud from the door.

Stop, sir! Come back! this instant, or, by Heaven!

I 'll mar your purpose!

Re-enter RICHARD.

Rich. [speaking with restrained passion.

What 's the matter now ?-

Osc. [*speaking eagerly and rapidly.*

    Promise me, sir, by all that you hold sacred,
You will do nothing against Manfred's life!
Swear it! no matter what may urge you! Swear it!
Swear! or you shall not quit the room this night.
Rich. I do. Now let me go. [*breaking away from him.*

              Osc. Go. But remember! [*hold-
                       ing him by the cuff.*
Dare harm him, and [*letting go.*] you die, sir, by my
  hand!

               [*Exit, precipitately, Richard.*
Osc. 'T is over! — Ah! — [*wiping his forehead.*

              God! what a fearful struggle!
The death-hour must have such a pang as that. —
Now I feel better — and my heart is lighter — [*sighing.*
My brother's blood will not lie on my soul. [*shuddering.*
He will not mind his fortune, — and his name,
What 's that to one who knows his heart is honest?
I am sweating still; [*again wiping his brow.*

           that minute's mental spasm
Has torn my nerves to pieces. [*Draws a chair to the
           table, and sits down as if to breathe.
      After a brief pause.*] Let me see.
I have bargain'd for his safety, in the event
This rude boy and himself encounter. Still,
By keeping Mattison beyond the hour,
I have given Manfred time to work his will.
If passion rule, he and his charmer fly —
Forever — for he has sworn it: this is best.

If caught in the street together, — that is well.
In either case, I must come up, in time
To jerk the wire of this good puppet Dick,
Who does my business, which he thinks his own,
And, like full many another passionate fool,
Will give to scandal his young sister's name.
And set his foot upon his father's heart, [*rising*.
To gratify revenge, perhaps some grudge,
Which he calls honor, but I know is — fudge!

> [*Begins to put on his cloak, and*
>
> *Scene closes.*

SCENE II.

The Square, as in Act III., Scene III.

The stage is still darker
than in the previous representation of the scene — indicating
the advance of the night.

Enter,

from the street that leads to Mattison's house,

MANFRED *and* HELEN.

They come forward. MANFRED *has his left hand laid*
lightly on HELEN's *waist, over her shawl, while*
his right holds her right hand.

Hel.   O go no further: it was here we parted;
And here we were to meet — to part again.
Manf. And part forever!   Was it not so sworn?
Hel.   And part — forever!
            She hesitates an instant, then
throws herself, in perfect abandonment of all self-restraint,
upon his shoulder and weeps.
                Manf. Helen!   Mercy!   Hush!
Now I have need of all my strength, do not,
Do not unman me thus, else I prove false
To God, to honor, to myself and thee!
O, it is madness in you thus to lean
Your head upon my shoulder!   I had thought

To wrestle with my own heart solely ; yours,
Yours too against my reason is too much.
Let us stand simply thus, your hand in mine.
Now hear me, Helen. I beheld the scene
Between you and your father, [*She starts and lays her
other hand over his, gazing in his face in
the extremity of surprise.*
— saw it all,
Through the half-clos'd shutter, and I vow'd to God
Those silver hairs should be to-night a veil
Between your beauty and my passion. [*She raises his
hand to her lips.*
Come;
Your father calls us, and the eyes of God
Look from the thousand stars to keep us chaste :
Come, while I yet can speak thus to you ! Come !
*He urges her gently on the way back,
in the same manner (his hand around her, &c.)
as they had entered.*
Hel. Yes, it is right to part. And yet ——
Manf. And yet ? —
*They have stopped, after taking
but a step or two ; and now* HELEN *again casts herself
on* MANFRED's *breast.*
Hel. O, I am lost to shame ! lost, lost, lost, lost !
Manf. Helen ! what is the matter ? Shame and you !
. [*pressing her to his breast.*
Hel. And is 't not bitter shame, when you are cold
And no more love me ——

Manf. Helen! [*in a tone of mourn-*
                          ful reproach.

Hel. [*without attending to the interruption.*
                     — as you did,
To own I dare not leave you? that I fear
To be alone now with my own wild thoughts?
O God, deliver me! the hour I have pass'd,
In waiting for this moment, I could not
Go through again, and live: and now, and now,
To think we never more shall meet again,
My heart will burst — I feel it, that it will;
And God grant only that it may be soon!

Manf. [*speaking with much agitation, while he gently*
           raises her head.

Helen! — And your poor father — that old man —
Must he die too? You shall live, for his sake;
And my kind cousin's cares, hers whom you love,
And who loves you so much, shall bring again
Peace to your innocent heart. Come, Helen, come.
                            [*They move off.*
Think of your father; it shall be——— Oh God!
              [*falling back, just as they have reach'd the*
                   mouth of the street.

Hel. [*in turn looking up the street.*

My brother! and my father! they have quit the
   house!

Desperately.] Take me now where you will — my
   name is gone!

Ever and ever!

Manf. [*catching her to his heart and kissing her.*
Ever and ever! for you are my *wife!*
Witness it God and Angels!   Now I dare
To kiss you.   Helen! [*looking on her anxiously.*
                 do not faint! bear up, [*untying*
                  the strings of her bonnet.
Yet but a little, and we shall be home. [*She falls across*
                       his arms.
Ah!   And the noise comes nearer!   Thus then, thus.
Lifts her in his arms, her bonnet
dropping to the ground, and her hair falling
in disorder about him, and runs with her to the street at the
left, nearest the proscenium.
Coachman! [*calling aloud, into the street.*
       Down with your steps there! triple fare!
       [*Exit, kissing Hel. rapturously, as he bears*
       her off in his arms.

Enter,
after a second or two, from the street
at the right corner, nearest the proscenium,
OSOAR.

Osc. That was my brother's lungs!   What, is he chas'd?
       [*turning his head toward the upper street on*
       the same side, and listening.
The hounds were close upon him: here they come.
I 'll whip them back to kennel, — though their legs
Would hardly overtake a coach and pair,
Whose driver is trebly fee'd.

Enter,
from the street of Mattison's house,
MARK MATTISON, RICHARD, *and* MEDDLEHAM.

MATTISON *and his son are without their hats or any overcoats.*

   Rich. [*furiously.*] Too late!
    Matt. [*despairingly.*] Too late!
Rich. But they shall not escape me! [*making for the very*
    quarter where Manf. and Hel. had actually
    disappeared.
    Osc. [*arresting him.*] And which way?
Without your hat too!
    Rich. [*struggling with him.*
    To the gates of Hell!
Osc. You 'll sooner reach it than you 'll gain on *them.*
Rich. Why do you stop me? Let go! But for you,
I had been in time.
    Osc. And but for me, I think,
You never would have known of this at all.
     [*Rich. ceases to struggle.*
I stop you; first, because *this* is the way —
    [*indicating the very street he himself had come*
    from, i. e., directly on a line, in an op-
    posite direction, with the true one.
 Stay! [*stopping Rich., who is about to take it.*
   — and because, even had the way been *that,*
You hardly would run faster than a coach,
A coach too paid for as my brother pays.
Besides, how could you see it in the dark?

Matt. My daughter! O my daughter!
                                        Rich. Since, it seems,
    You saw all this, why did you let them 'scape?
Osc. [*haughtily.*

        Perhaps because I chose it. — But, good sir,
    Am I the Devil, or a steam-machine,
    To stop a coach that 's running, with my thumb?
    The parties too unwilling, man and maid,
    She kissing him and urging him to speed?
Matt. Miserable child! Lost! lost!
                                        Rich. Curse on her!
                                        Matt. Hush!
Medd. [*who has been curiously turning over Helen's hat
        with his stick.*

    Whose bonnet 's this has fallen in the street?
Matt. Helen's! Give, give it to me! 't is my child's.
Rich. No! [*snatching it from Medd., and flinging it from
    him.*] Damn it! let it lie in the street, to rot,
    Or serve some strumpet's head less vile than hers!
Osc. [*severely, and taking Rich. by the arm.*

    Young man, respect at least your parent's years,
    If you have no compassion for his woes.
                    *Picks up the bonnet, brushes it
    gently with his handkerchief as if to clean it of the dust,
        and hands it deprecatingly to* MATTISON.

    Take it, thou good old man, nor be asham'd
    To treasure it in memory of your child.
    Perhaps too she is not so vile. This hat,
    Abandon'd thus, looks little like free will.

Though reconcil'd at last, and urging flight,
My wicked brother must have forc'd her off.   ʼ
Matt. God bless you, sir! the world has done you wrong.
Medd. Ay, and your joke to-night did not correct it.
The next time you assume another's name,
Pray let it be a better than your own.
You are not Manfred, and, though rough, are true,
And, had your threats been kicks, you still should find,
An upright heart has made amends for all.

[shaking his hand.

Osc. I know not what you mean: but sure, the Devil
Himself might reverence these silver hairs.
But come, the night-air is not good for them;
And if we stay much longer in this place,
[10] So queerly rigg'd and with such troubled mien,
A mob will be upon us. See already,
Where some fool lifts a window over head.

[looking up to one of the houses, where a head
is now seen looking out.

Rich. But what do you propose to do? [sulkily.

Osc. Even this:

To meet you at my uncle's house forthwith.
Manfred he loves, but never honors knaves;
And he will aid you to a prompt redress.
But first go home and cover that white head,

[gently touching Rich.

And shield that body from the pitiless cold,
And put your own hat on; then, with all haste,
Go to Sir Henry's — not yourself alone,

But your ag'd father, and this worthy friend.
All must be present.   You will find me there.
    RICHARD *takes his father by the arm,*
  who, ever since he received HELEN's *hat, has*
  been standing in a mute abstraction, gazing on it,
    as if he were silently weeping, and Exit with
          him down the street.
Medd. [*stepping behind to shake Oscar's hand.*
    Good-by till then — to meet, much better friends.
              [*Exit.   And the inquisitive neighbor*
                    shuts down the window.
Osc. [*alone.*] Ay, my old cock? · And yet an hour ago
  I was about to wring your neck!   'T was then,
  When I was true, though rough, because I tried
  To give you a bloody comb, your spurs were rais'd
  And your short feathers bristling round your wattles:
  Now I am really dangerous — not more false
  Saffise's fingers when they sign the cross —
  You cackle delicate as a dunghill-hen
  That has laid an egg beside a lump of chalk!
  So *fair-and-softly* wins some kindly fools,
  While others, like that boy, are devilish shrewd
  In spying out faith beneath a satyr's mask!
Moves onward toward the street where MANFRED *and* HELEN
          made their Exeunt.
    And now to triumph, [*adjusting the collar of his cloak.*
              and end a good day's work.
      Stops a moment, and looks upward.
  "Ye stars! which are the poetry of Heaven " —

As writes some great ass— Byron, I believe—
Though one and all, compris'd the planets seven,
Look more like fish-scales shining through a sieve, —
At least to me, who, by such mystic phrases,
Am taught fire sings and human diction blazes, —
Ye stars, beneath whose ever-twinkling eyes
Manfred has play'd the fool, and I heen wise,
Shine on, for other lovers like my brother,
And let their joy be still to hug each other,
That wiser men may thence good profit draw,
And cull the clean wheat while they thresh the straw !
Manfred has gone with Helen to be blest.
Amen! while, bidding you a bright unrest,

       [lifting his hat and bowing with mock
              reverence toward the sky.

I— but my rhymes run out! In sober prose,
I go, to lead—my uncle by the nose.

                       [Exit.

SCENE III. AND THE LAST.

Same as in Act I., Scene I.

The chandelier, or other lamp suspended from the ceiling, is lighted up.

SIR HENRY *and* VINCENT.

[11] *Sir H.* We seem to have the parlor to ourselves!
In waiting those rude boys, and Sybil too,
What say you, Vincent, to a game of chess?
Vin. With all my heart, Sir Henry; but 't would be
Only begun, to be abandon'd soon.·
With the first move, your lovely niece appears,
And what becomes then of our rooks and knights?
Sir. H. True; though you held my king himself in check,
I verily think you would resign the board
At the first rustle of the beauty's gown.
Why, how you blush! I sometimes half-suspect
You really love the sprightly widow better
Than Manfred does himself. Tut, tut! that heart
                    [*touching Vin. playfully on the breast.*
Is not so sage, man, as its owner's head.
'T is well it 's honest; Manfred's else might quake.
But as for Sybil's company just now,
A carriage drove np as I pass'd the hall:
Whom it contain'd I know not, but my niece
Was summon'd by her maid, on some affair
Of private nature. Doubtless 't is a visit

For some beneficent object, where her name
Stands always foremost.

                     Vin. As an angel's should.
The odor of good deeds is carried far.
Despite of secrecy, each act takes wind,
And thousands rush to gather from the tree
Celestial, that in human garden blooms, —
Perennial growth! but planted wide between.

Sir. H. Bravo! that poetry and panegyric
    Shall take wind too, like Charity's own flower,
    And bear its odors to the " angel's " ear.

Vin. For Heaven's sake, no, Sir Henry! She mocks ever
    My best-turn'd compliments, and calls them dull.

Sir H. You silly fellow! 't is because they please.
    You 're a rare judge of women! Is he not? [*turning
                    round, as he hears the door open.*

              Enter OSCAR.

Oh! [*as if he had expected some one else.*
    —Where the deuse, fair nephew, have you been?

Osc. [*looking significantly, but without impertinence, at Vin.*
    To see how courage well becomes a sage,
    To find even fools grow wise when madmen rage,
    To feel how easily the headstrong fall,
    And learn one meddler may confound them all.

Sir. H. Oracular quite! But please, sir, to explain
    The riddle of these Delphic rhymes.

                    Osc. Not while
So rare a secret-fathomer stands here.

Try his long plummet, uncle.

     Sir. H. What is this? [*looking
from one to the other in amazement.*
What means this madcap, Mr. Vincent? Say.

Vin. Pardon me, sir, I cannot gloss a muse
I find so seldom friendly, as is his.

Osc. And yet you might, for on my honor, sir,
I spoke a compliment, and meant it too.
But [*shrugging his shoulders.*] — as you like.

A murmur of voices heard at the door by which OSCAR *had
entered.   It is then thrown open suddenly.*

     Sir. H. What novel guests are these?

Rich. [*speaking without, while Meddleham is seen coming in.*
We stand in need of no announcement here:

       Enter,

after MEDDLEHAM, MATTISON, — RICHARD *supporting him
by the arm, and still speaking.*

We come for justice.

    Medd. Justice.

      Matt. And my child.

  Instantly, as the words are said,

       Enter,

from the opposite side, HELEN, *between* MANFRED *and* SYBIL,
*who have, each of them, a hand of hers,
while* SYBIL'S *is also round her waist.* HELEN'S
*hair is modestly arranged. She has no shawl, but is otherwise
in the dress in which she met* MANFRED.

The whole company present are
thrown into agitation. SIR HENRY
looks confounded ; VINCENT *surprised, yet*
anxious ; OSCAR *seems crest-fallen,* MEDDLEHAM
perplexed, while MATTISON *stretches out his arms to*
his daughter, who makes toward him, and RICHARD *seems*
unable to move, between purposed revenge and amaze-
ment at the strange turn matters seem to have
taken. VINCENT, *however, moves near to*
him, as if to prevent difficulty.

Hel. [*rushing into her father's arms.*

Father!

  Matt. [*tenderly, yet holding her off, while he gazes*
    inquiringly in her face.

  My child!

    Rich. [*vehemently to Manfred.*

    Explain, sir.

      Manf. [*calmly, and with a*
    slight gesture, turning the palm of his hand
      toward him, as if to wave him back.

      In a moment.

Rich. [*with increased vehemence.*

I claim redress.

    Matt. [*holding Helen in his arms, as she*
      hangs upon his shoulder.

  I ask but for my child.

Manf. [*moving toward Mattison.*

Both shall be answer'd.   But I claim my wife.

A new movement in the company.
VINCENT *seems surprised, but still more*
sad; SYBIL *goes up to* SIR HENRY, *takes his*
hand, and appears to intercede and expostulate with
him; OSOAR *seems to restrain a movement of despair;* MED
DLEHAM *goes up nearer to* MANFRED, *contemplating him*
with interest; RICHARD *stands irresolute and*
half-incredulous, looking from HELEN *to*
MANFRED *attentively, while* MATTISON
starts from HELEN'S *embrace.*

Sir H. Ah!

    Vin. Fatal rashness!

                Matt. Heavens! — Helen! — Speak![12]
         [*holding her from him, and gazing on her,*
                          and from her to
                               Manfred.

Manf. [*smiling.*

    Speak, Helen; and now say, — whose claim is best?
       He spreads out his hands to her,
    and HELEN, *for answer, rushes into his arms and*
         he folds her to his breast.

    Yes, sir, [*extending his left hand to Rich., his right*
                       being still round Hel.

    I carried off your sister: 't was,
    As I repeat, to make her truly mine. [*Rich. touches*
                     his hand, but coldly.

                     You, sir,
                        [*to Matt.*

    Ask'd but your child, and you have twice your wish;

For are you not my father too, as hers?
> [*Releasing Helen, he gives his hand to the old man,
> who presses it in both of his with great emotion.*

Matt. How could I doubt you?

> *Medd.* And the world speaks true.
> [*following, with evident admiration, Manf., as
> the latter walks up, diffidently, to his uncle.*

Manf. Uncle, forgive me; you alone I have wrong'd.

Sir H. Unhappy boy! 't is not of me alone,
Whose hopes you have so cruelly deceiv'd,
You have to ask forgiveness, but yourself.
This girl, though lovely, and, I doubt not, good,
Is not your match, in birth nor in estate.

Medd. Pardon, Sir Henry; but she is, in both.

Sir H. Sir! Who are you, pray?

> *Medd.* I 'm Ralph Meddleham.

They spell me Meddle-ham; but people say
Middleum always, and I say so too.

> *During the dialogue between*
> SIR HENRY *and* MANFRED, HELEN,
> *at* SYBIL's *motion, has led her up to her
> father, and an introduction takes place in
> dumb show, with marks of great cordiality on both
> sides. Then* SYBIL, *with her own hands, draws an armchair
> near the old man, and would have him sit in it, but
> he declines with a firm and somewhat lofty air;
> and, with her on one side and* HELEN *on
> the other, stands and listens, with
> the rest of the company, to
> what follows.*

[18] *Sir H.* Middleum? — Ah! [*seeming to recall something,
and looking attentively at Medd.*

Medd. Your eldest brother ——

Sir H. Well!

Medd. Marry'd a lady of the name of Calvert.
She was the daughter of my father's niece.

Sir H. [*extending his hand frankly.*

Sir, you are welcome. Though we are not kin,
I lov'd my brother, and am glad to see
The cousin of his wife.

Medd. [*shaking his hand.*] 'T is kindly said.
Manfred, you are my cousin twice remov'd,
Yet are more near, by all that I have heard,
And which this night confirms, near to my heart
Than brothers to each other always are.
Give me your honest hand. And your hand too:

[*to Oscar, with whom however he shakes
hands less cordially.*

'T is better thus than kicks and broken bones.

Osc. Much; but a jolly way that was of yours,
Tumbling into acquaintance on one's back!

[*Sir H. and Manf. exchange momentary
looks of slight surprise.*

Sir. H. Pardon me, that I venture to remind you
Of your first theme. What has all this to do
With the young lady Manfred would espouse?

Medd. The same blood, that has mixed with yours in his,
Has mingled with Mark Mattison's in hers:
Her grand-aunt was my mother. Pretty Helen,

Have you no welcome for your father's cousin?
approaching her, she advancing to him.
And the group, following MEDDLEHAM, *is thus*
made to gather about MATTISON. MEDDLEHAM *takes*
HELEN'S *hand, and puts a hand upon her head*
admiringly and affectionately.
Sir Henry, I have no one in the world
To love as kin, save those I have round me now;
And I am very rich, — so people say.
Where shall I then find heirs, if 't is not here?
Thus much for Helen's wealth. As for her birth,
To-morrow cousin Mark will make it clear
That fallen fortune is but fall'n estate,
And that his cradle was such wood as yours.
Sir H. Manfred, though Helen had been lowly born,
And poor as lowly, I had learn'd in time
To grow contented, happy that my boy
Had not forgot his honor in his love,
Nor made a wreck of innocence for pride.
But now the world too must approve your choice;
And since you wish it, be it so, my son.
OSCAR *moving upward, and consequently apart from*
the group, seems to suffer an emotion of pain.
Yet, well you know, my heart was set elsewhere.
Manf. Then let me, for that heart's sake as for mine,
Beg for another your best interest here.
Taking SYBIL'S *hand, just as she turns away, and*
reaching with his other hand to VINCENT, *and leading him down.*
Who in this world is worthy Sybil's love,

But Vincent, my true friend?

        Sir H. And next yourself,

              [Oscar returns, with fresh interest, and
                      listens anxiously.

Whom would I sooner gift with such a prize?

      [looking inquiringly to Sybil, who betrays
                emotion and confusion.

Vin. With such a sanction—might I *[agitated and em-*
    barrassed.] — dare aspire?——

Syb. Sir I—*[Then, shaking off all embarrassment by a sud-*
    den effort, and placing her hand with a
    noble frankness and sweet dignity
    in Vincent's.

'T is to stoop to such a heart and hand.
A man of Mr. Vincent's matchless faith
Might dare aspire to win an empress' love.

    VINCENT *presses her hand to his heart*
and lips. The company gather round them, and they
are parted, MANFRED *taking* VINCENT'S *hand, while* OSCAR,
beyond the circle, clasps his hands passionately
together, and bites his lips.

Manf. [*in an under tone to Vin.*
    And *did* win Sybil Vernon's long ago.

Vin. Ah I [*looking earnestly at Manf.*
    He then, turning round, and seeing the
company engaged in mutual congratulation and
introductions of the strangers to one another, &c., &c
draws MANFRED *aside, or down the scene,*
close to the footlights.

Tell me, frankly, was it for my sake,
Dear Manfred, you were cold to Sybil's charms?
Manf. Why, man, you lov'd her: where was need of two?
Vin. How could I be so blind? You generous soul!
                              [*pressing both his hands.*
Manf. You would not have me be outdone by you!
Yours was the lesson.
                    Vin. And you learn'd it well.
              They rejoin the rest, where SIR HENRY
has just placed old MATTISON *in the chair he had before
refused.* VINCENT *takes* SYBIL'S *hand with a
movement of gratitude and deep affection.*
Hel. Now I am happier. [*to Sybil.*
          Syb. [*smiling.*] What! and was there room?

                    Enter SAFFISE,
*with muff, shawl, and hat, dressed coquettishly,
but according to her station.* OSCAR, *observing her first,
darts forward to remove her.*

Sir H. [*attracted by the movement.*
          What 's this?
                    Hel. Saffise! [*in astonishment, exchanging
                    looks with her father and brother, while, by
                    pressing nearer to Manf., she seems also
                    to fear.*
                    Osc. Begone!
                              Saff. Not till I 'm heard.
Sir H. What is the matter?
                    Osc. 'T is a silly girl ——

Saff. Silly in trusting to a heartless villain, —
But not so silly as to kiss the rod
When she has strength to give back blow for blow —-
As you shall find! [*poising herself on her toes, and
gesticulating as on a former occasion.*
Osc. [*affecting wonder and commiseration.*
The creature 's mad! — Come out!
[*seizes her by the arm.*
Medd. [*interfering.*
Mad? *Irish* mad then: she seems far more angry.
Saff. That is it, sir: I 'm in a furions rage! [*clenching her
fist* (but without raising the arm) *with
ludicrous passion.*
You are Sir Henry Ferguson, I think;
[*moving up to Sir H.*
You will not shut your ears to me, nor suffer
This dirty wretch, because he is your nephew,
To abuse me — and yourself — and Helen there —
And ——
Osc. [*menacing.*
Devil! will you hold your tongue?
Rich. [*eagerly approaching Saff.*] Speak on!
Sir H. Oscar, stand back; and you, yonng sir, have pa-
tience.
I am the one address'd : permit me then.
My girl, if you have anything to say,
Follow me to a fitter place. This way. [*indicating to
her to follow him out.*
Saff. No sir, this is the fittest place. 'T is here,

Where it so happens that I see around me
All that are most concern'd to know this truth,
That I shall tell it.   Learn, your nephew there,
That Oscar! has been seeking, by my help,
To undermine his truer-hearted brother.
In your esteem, and ruin that young girl,
Who, I had thought, by this time would have been
In a different house from this. —

       Rich. By Heaven!—
       [*making a step toward Oscar.*
        Matt. Richard!
Remember where you are, my son.
       Osc.. Sir Henry,
This is some villain's plot; the girl is hired.
You will not suffer such a hussy ——
       Saff. Hussy!
And who has made me so?   I am none but yours.
The plot is yours, the villain is yourself;
And for the hire, it was to hold my tongue.
You had better hold your own; those ugly names,
That save your brother, lose you an estate.
Sir Henry, I am come to face this shame,
Although it is more dreadful than I fear'd,
For some are here that never thought me bad.
    [*with a moment's glance at the Mattisons.*
     Then, casting down her eyes.
I am his mistress.   Let the horrid pain,
Of owning it in the ears of such as these,
Make some atonement for my being such.

This very afternoon, did he induce me
To inveigle that young girl into my rooms,
Whither he was to make his brother come,
And did, that Helen's weakness might be ——
                    Manf. [*sternly.*] Hush!
Uncle, let her not say another word.

Rich. She has said enough: I have proof of it. Come out.
            [*to Osc., touching him smartly on the arm, as*
                he passes him on his way to the door.

Manf. [*arresting Rich.*

    Mattison — Richard — brother! For my sake,
Whom doubtless you have thought too harshly of, —
For Helen's — for your father's! ——
                    Vin. And for mine.
                            [*gravely.*
Young man, you owe me some amends, for words
Spoken injuriously, you well know where.
Make them, by letting your own wrongs go by.

Matt. Richard, — I do command you! [*Rich. hesitates.*
                    Syb. And I, sir,
If you will let me, I — entreat you.

She takes him by the fingers, and leads him, scarce resisting,
                to his father's chair.
            Osc. [*who has watched the whole proceeding with*
                his arms folded.

                            Oh!
Good people, this was pains superfluous:
I will not harm the lad.

Rich. [*endeavoring to escape.*] It is too much!

Matt. [*who holds him by the wrist.*

    The greater merit then in your endurance.
Stand still, my son.

                Sir H. Obey your parent, sir;
And I, at least, will own you are a man.

He lays his hand flatteringly on RICHARD's *shoulder, who
bows, and resists no longer.*

Medd. 'T is your first step in wisdom, — and well planted.
I like you better now than I had hop'd. [*shaking
                      Richard's hand.*

Osc. Well, I am glad the gentleman has gain'd
Something at least he never had before.
I shall not put to test his new discretion.

Sir H. Silence! for shame at least. [*severely.*

              Osc. [*without in the least
            regarding his uncle's interruption.*

              The more so too,
That I have similar matter on my hands,
And much more weighty. You will not forget?

              [*significantly to Vincent.*

Manf. [*rapidly, and preventing Vincent from replying.*

    Ah! I remember. Brother, it would seem,
You have done, or sought to do me, grievous wrong;
Why I know not, nor do I ask to know.
If you would have me to forgive you ——

            Osc. [*haughtily.*] First,
Wait till I ask you.

        Manf. As a favor then,
Do not pursue this silly quarrel further.

And you, my friend [*to Vin.*]—— But I am sure of you.

Osc. [*carelessly.*

Well, I am no wise anxious for the sport.

I have tried his mettle, and he well knows mine :

If he have no wish to pursue it further ? ——

Vin. [*coldly.*

It never was a quarrel of my seeking.

Osc. Then we are quits.— And now for Texas. Saff,

[*gaily,*

What say you ? will you thither?

Saff. But you jest?

Osc. Jest?   Not a whit of it !   Plainly, will you come ?

Saff. [*after looking at him steadily for a moment.*

I will. [*Gives her hand boldly to Osc. to lead her out.*

The company evince extreme surprise,

mixed with pain.

Manf. [*going up to her anxiously.*

You cannot mean it !

Sir H. Are you mad?

Saff. No, sir ; not now, no more than I was then.

I know your nephew, and he knows me — well.

He dares not touch me.

Osc. And he has no wish —

At least in a hostile way. I' faith, you puss !

I like you all the better for your claws.

We shall make our fortunes still. Who knows ? perhaps

Some day may see me in the Governor's chair !

And when I am, you vixen, I may make

Saffise perhaps my—— [*pausing.   The company
start.   Hel. even moves a step toward him,
and Saffise herself, with evident emotion, grasps his arm.*
— Secretary of State.

Hel. [*timidly.*]

Saffise,— do stay; and be to me a —— [*attempting
to take her hand.*

Saff. [*roughly.*] What?

A foil to the splendor which I see awaits you?
No! never again in this accursed town
Will I set foot.   Don't touch me! [*stamping, and draw-
ing back.*

for I hate you!

Hel. [*still timidly, yet sadly.*

Hate me, Saffise?   I never did you wrong.

Saff. [*fiercely.*

And are you not then happy? [*Hel. falls back, in
amazement, upon Syb. and Manf., who have
approached to remove her from Saff.*

Manf. Come away: [*gently
to Hel., and in a low tone.*

She will not understand you.

Saff. Ah! too well.

But — pity! and from her! ——

With a broken utterance.] Sir — Mr. Ferguson —
[*pauses, casting down her eyes.*

Manf. [*gently.*] Say then: can I do aught for you, my girl?

Saff. [*her whole manner altered — her voice dejected — and
her eyes still cast down.*
Will you permit me, sir — to — touch your hand ? —
If you will take the hand of — one like me.

MANFRED *secretly slides a purse of
money into his hand ere he extends it to her, which he does
frankly, and with an air of great compassion,
and even consideration.*

Manf. Why not ? [*in a mild, low tone.*
I never scorn the unfortunate.
Saff. Then,
Heaven bless you ! [*raising his hand passionately to
her lips.*
But not this. [*offering back the purse.*
— And yet [*hesitating.*
— and yet —
It may be well to have it with me too :
An amulet, more precious than my cross,
'T will be to this bad bosom, — and perhaps,
To have it there, my heart will beat the happier.
[*Kisses it and puts it into her bosom.*
Perchance a day may come too, when this gold
May save the Creole from — a natural fate,
And a deserv'd one you may think.   Farewell !
[*with much emotion.*
Osc. [*who has made one or two impatient turns while she
has been addressing Manf., and at last faced her
with a sarcastic look.*
VOL. IV.—6*

Well play'd, Melpomenè! — Good people, all,
    [*bowing with his hat around the assembly.*
Farewell! [*mimicking Saffise's heart-broken tone.*
Turns to Manf.] With my share, added to your own,
Of uncle's leavings, brother, you 'll be rich.
Pray don't forget the Muses, — nor to add
(In your next acquisitions in the Arts),
In honor of your studies in the Square,
Cupid and Psyche to your classic groups.
Sir H. [*who has been regarding him with more and more
    indignation.*

Or say, have Power to cut him Satan, sneering
Over the joy of Adam with his Eve.
Osc. [*bowing to Sir H.*
    Adam had no fool-uncle, I believe.
                    [*Exit, with Saff.*
· *Sir H.* Miserable boy!
            Manf. [*rushing after them.*
              O, do not let them go!
Oscar! [*calling after him.*
Sir H. [*stopping Manf. and pressing his hand.*
'T is better as it is, my son.
Is it not, Mr. Vincent?
            Vin. Yes, for both.
Even could Oscar face his friend again,
Manfred would grieve, conceiving in his brother
A self-remorse perhaps he never felt.
MANFRED *moves pensively to* HELEN, *who is by her father's
    side, and takes her hand.*

Matt. And you, my daughter, what have you escap'd!

A nature so perverted as that girl's!

. Not wholly bad; but even its virtues such,

As to make dangerous her will to evil:

'T was perilous such a contact, even for once!

Hel. [*humbly.*] Thank God then, I am no more in its reach:

It is my fortune, more than my desert.

Matt. Nay, not so, Helen; for that were to say,

That innocence cries up to Heaven in vain.

Who should be heard there, if not you? Kneel down.

I blest you when your heart was breaking; now

That you are happiest of all womankind,

God keep you blest, my good, my tender child!

Manf. And have you not a blessing too for me,

My father? [*bowing his head before the old man.*

    Matt. [*laying his hand upon Manfred's head.*

    Thou art blest already, son.

Thou noble Manfred! to a man like thee

What dower can equal such a heart as hers!

Pure thou hast kept her; pure she will remain;

For men like thee stain not the thing they love,

And even their joys have still some smack of Heaven.

Vin. 'T is truly spoke!

    Syb. And Manfred's virtuous soul

Has earn'd its joy by conquest over self.

Manf. Praise my will only; here lay all my power.

    [*placing his hand reverentially on the old man's*

      locks.   All but Helen look surprised.

Yes, when you learn the story of my strife

With lust and pride, and how I won my wife,
The conquest, you will find I rightly said,
Was owing all to this dear SILVER HEAD.

*As he speaks this, MANFRED, being
on the old man's right, has one hand
gently laid on his venerable locks, while the
other, his right, is in MATTISON's right hand;
HELEN, now risen, is on her father's left, and in the
same attitude, saving that she presses the old man's hair
to her lips, gathering up a cluster of the silver locks
from his shoulder. The company, on either side
of this principal group, are arranged according to the nearness of their inter-
ests in either MANFRED or HELEN.*

The Curtain falls

upon the picture.

NOTES

NOTES

THE SILVER HEAD

1.—P. 10. *Quiting* —] The compositor having doubled the *t* in this word, supposing it an error of *copy*, it occurs to me that it may be well to observe I mean the *i* should be pronounced long; *quiting* of *Quite*, not *quitting* of *Quit*. They are the same word. And there is no reason why there should not be *Quite* as well as *Re-quite*, in the sense in which they are synonymous, if it be only for the uses of the poet, and to keep it in this usage distinct from *Quit*. It will be found again in the *Double Deceit*, Act IV., Sc. 2. — Chaucer so wrote and sounded the word.

> "And she that helmed was in starke stonres,
> And wan by force tounes stronge and toures,
> Shal on hire hed now were a vitremite:
> And she that bare the sceptre ful of floures,
> Shal bere a distaf hire cost for to *quits*."
> *The Monkes Tale.*
> (*C. T.* ed. TYRWHITT. cr. 8vo. *Lond.* 1830. V. III. p. 172.)

> "Ye gon to Canterbury; God yon spede,
> The blisful martyr *quite* you your mede."
> *Prol. to C. T. ib.* I. p. 81.

> "I can a noble tale for the nones.
> With which I wol now *quite* the knightes tale."
> *The Milleres Prologue.* ib. IL D. L

And just before, on the same page, we have *quiten* :

> "Now telleth ye, sire Monk, if that ye conne,
> Somewhat, to quiten with [*wherewith to quite*] the knightes tale."

I find also in one of my dictionaries a marginal reference to *The Old Law*, Act II., Sc. 2; but I cannot now verify the citation.

In the mouth of *Manfred,* "quite" for "requite" is not an improbable expression, while "quit," in the same sense, would be both affected and unnatural. But the Actor may read *quitting,* if he will.

2.—P. 12.   — *or left* —] That is, the *right,* as the audience sits. — And so, throughout these volumes; *right* and *left* being always in reference to the Actor's position, as he faces the assemblage.

Further, I may here observe, for those unfamiliar with the phraseology of the theatre, that *up* or *upward* in the stage-directions means backward from the audience, while *down* or *downward* is towards the audience. — This also, throughout the volumes.

3.—P. 49.   *Why this is capital!* etc.] The stress of the voice in *Manfred's* part is on "is":

> "Why this is capital!   M. What *is'* so?   O. This—"

If it he laid on "What," where it would fall more naturally, though not so elegantly, *Oscar's* part must begin "*Why* this":

> "Why this is capital!   M. What' is so?   O. Why, this—'

4.—P. 54.   *Most strange indeed, a man so keenly quick* —] For the Stage, "Very strange, a man, *etc.*"; which, though slightly defective in metre, is the proper reading, and in fact the original one.

5.—P. 57. He touches Saffise on the shoulder, *etc.*, *etc.*] This pantomime takes place while *Manfred* and *Helen* are conversing, but is very brief.

6.—P. 71. *Whether the book*—] For the Stage, omit from here to "and."

7.—P. 72. *Bless her*—] From here, five verses to be omitted.

8.—P. 75. *Whose delicate freshness*, etc.] Omit this verse.

9.—P. 75. *And yet*—] Omit all of the soliloquy after these words.

10.—P. 110. *So queerly*, etc.] Omit this line.

11.—P. 113. Sir H. *etc.*] Omit ten verses, commencing "Why, how you blush!"

12.—P. 117. Sir H. *Ah!* Vin. *Fatal rashness!* Matt. *Heavens! —Helen!— Speak!*] These three parts (*Sir H.*, *Vin.*, and *Matt.*) are spoken nearly simultaneously, and instantly after *Manfred's* "I claim my wife."

13.—P. 119. *Middleum*, etc., to *Her grandaunt was*, etc.] In the original MS. is the following reading for these nineteen verses. But that of the text is preferable. The choice is with the Theatre.

> *Sir H.* Middleum — Ah! [*seeming to recollect something, and look- ing earnestly on Medd.*
> *Medd.* Your eldest brother's daughter ——
> *Sir H.* Elop'd with a young fellow of that name ——
> *Medd.* Who was an honest fellow not the less,
> Being the Ralph, but no more young, before you.
> [*Oscar moves nearer to the group, and shows great interest.*

Sir H. You are my niece's husband, then?

       Medd. I was;
But not so poor a man, nor yet so mean,
As to be anxious to assert the tie.

Sir H. Tut! you mistake: you are most heartily welcome.

          [extending his hand.
You may believe me, for I boast to be
Frank as your cousin Manfred who stands here.

Medd. Now, that is kind. [*shaking Sir H.'s hand cordially.*

      And, cousin, your hand too. [*to Manf.*
'T is better this [*to Osc., with a similar action, but less hearty.*
  than kicks and broken bones.

Osc. Much. But a jolly way that was of yours,
To pounce into acquaintance on one's back.

    [Sir H. and Manf. exchange looks of slight surprise.

Sir H. And there 's another cousin still of yours. [*indicating*

          Sybil with a nod.
But first, what has this all to do with Helen?

SYBIL *coming forward gives her hand frankly*
to MEDD., *who takes it cordially and with marked*
    admiration and surprise.

Medd. A cousin this, worth traveling far to see.

Syb. [*smiling.*] That by and by: pray speak of Helen now.

Medd. Who is to me much nearer than you all;
For the same blood runs in the veins of both.
Her grandaunt was, *etc.*

THE DOUBLE DECEIT

OR

THE HUSBAND-LOVERS'

MDCCCLVI

CHARACTERS, ETC.

FRANCESCO FOSCARI, *Doge of Venice.*

MARCO FOSCARI, *his brother, Procurator of St. Mark.*

ALOÏSE[2] FOSCARI, *Marco's son.*

ANSELMO BARBADICO,
GIROLAMO BEMBO, } *Venetian gentlemen.*
GIOVANNI MORO,

PIETRO LOREDANO, *Admiral of the Venetian fleet.*

STEFANO MOCENIGO, *of the Council of Ten.*

DOMENICO MARIPETRO, *a "Signor of the Night."*

A CAPTAIN *of the "Signors of the Night."*

His LIEUTENANT.

A CHAPLAIN.

*His brother-*PRIEST.

Two SURGEONS.

A GONDOLIER.

ISOTTA, *wife of Anselmo.*

LUTIA, *wife of Girolamo.*

GISMONDA, *a young and noble widow, daughter of Giovanni
Moro.*

CASSANDRA, *Isotta's maid.*

GIOVANNA, *Lutia's maid.*

GIULIETTA, *Gismonda's maid.*

An OLD WOMAN.

Mute Personages

Members of the COUNCIL OF TEN. — SIX COUNSELORS *of the
Doge; Members of the* CRIMINAL QUARANTI'A; *and
other bodies forming the* COLLEGE.

A LAYBROTHER. — SBIRRI (archers of the day and night police).

A JAILER.

_____

SCENE. *Venice, in the middle of the 15th century.*

THE DOUBLE DECEIT

SCENE I.   *A garden.   Across the scene, a low hedge of twisted reeds, dividing it into two.*

Enter,
quickly, from the right (in the foreground),
ISOTTA.

She trips along the hedge, and looking over it to the right, claps her hands.

Isot. Come, Lutia! come, duck! now our bears are gone. —
To herself.] Little she dreams what sport is in the wind!

Enter LUTIA,
also from the right, but on the other side of the hedge.

Lut. [*kissing her.*

  What wast thou saying, Isotta mine?

           Isot. O what?
The old prayer, surely; that the Lord would please
Convert the un-Christian hearts of our two lords, —
Or break them — since thou, Lutia dear, and I
Have too much heart to do it — as we might.

Lut. Yes, as we might.

       Isot. Ah! say'st thou? Now, I wonder
If with like cause. — But is it not a shame, ·
We foster-sisters, and dear-loving friends,
Should have our bodies parted — not our souls —
By house-walls, or a garden-hedge as now,
Because, forsooth! in John Soranza's time, —
Or my own ancestor's, for aught I know,
Doge Gradenigo, — our good lords' bad foresires,
Having less brains than mettle, and strong hands,
Chose to break one another's heads.

         Lut. So we,
Poor innocent girls, who married their descendants,
Must live two years close neighbors, and not see
The inside of each other's homes!

        Isot. What if
Our lords reserv'd that privilege for themselves?

Lut. Of seeing each other's houses?

        Isot. Ay. I know
Of one at least who is so curious.

        Lut. I
As well.

Isot. Thou? Talk'st thou thus again? But come!
Leap thou thy neighbor's hedge: Cassandra keeps
Excellent watch at home.

LUTIA, *bringing a footstool to the side of the hedge, steps over
it with the assistance of* ISOTTA.

> So. — [*They embrace and
> come forward.*

> Did she not,

My spouse would think this trespass nought to one
That I might tell him of, had I a mind.

Lut. And so might mine, change but the side o' the hedge —
Had I a mind.

> *Isot.* Hadst thou a mind? Indeed!

Why what has thou to plain of, gentle dove?

Lut. As much as thou 't may be, if not the same.

Isot. Well, to the proof. Thou 'lt sorely be surpris'd,
Angry perhaps at first.

> *Lut.* And so wilt thou.

Isot. But then thou 'lt laugh, I think.

> *Lut.* And so wilt thou.

Isot. Thy lord——

> *Lut.* Thy lord ——

> > *Isot.* Giro'lamo——

> > > *Lut.* Anselmo——

Isot. Has——

> *Lut.* Has——

> > *Isot.* Made love to me.

> > > *Lut.* Made love to me.

Isot. Thou jest'st. My lord, the haughty and severe! ——

Lut.   Messer Anselmo Barbadico——

                           Isot. Has!——

Lut.   Made love, not haughty nor severe, to me.

     ISOTTA *looks at her for a moment confounded,*
       then bursts into a peal of laughter.

Isot.   Why, Lutia darling, this is double sport!

     I came to make thee laugh and cry at once

     At thy lord's impudence; and now, behold,

     I freeze and thaw in turn, to hear of mine!

     The Devil is in the men!

                    Lut. Perhaps they think

     The Devil 's in us.

             Isot. That well may be for me.

     The gay and gallant hairbrain'd cavalier,

     Messer Girolamo, hopes to find sure game

     In such another rattle as himself.

     But what does grave Anselmo see to doubt

     In such a sober, gentle thing as thou?

Lut.   He takes me for still water like himself.

Isot.   But if he has mistaken thy depth, my dear,

     We have sounded his: and that we 'll show anon.

     Now, were we like some Venice fair I know,

     Our lords might suffer somewhat, might they not?

Lut.   Now, Heaven forbid!   That were to prove ourselves

     Worthy the wrong they do us, or would do.

     No, my Isotta, let us shame these men

     By showing we are above them.

                   Isot. So I mean.

     But we will punish too.   What! when they smite

One of our cheeks, and we, as Christ bids, turn
The other to them also, shall we not
Show by the redness where the blow was given?
We will, and call like color into theirs.
                             Lut. But not
By striking.
               Isot. Only a love-pat. But first ——
How long since my insatiate lord devoured
With ogre eyes thy beauty? Did he more?
Lut. With ogling eyes, thou mean'st. He did no more.
And 't was enough to do, for two whole weeks,
In street, and church, casino, and where not.
Isot. For two whole weeks! Thou lowly, shrinking violet!
I knew my queenly roses were more priz'd.
For one whole month thy more judicious master
Has tried to bring them nearer to his eyes.
Lut. How know'st thou that?
                   Isot. By trying, simple lady:
As thou didst, I suppose. At first, surprise
Made me distrust the Signor Bembo's eyes.
But seeing them shine, and with no devious ray,
Upon his neighbor's garden, day by day,
I fear'd the truth, and so, to probe my fear,
Stoop'd once my delicate flower-stalk more near.
In other words, one morn, when full of fun,
I look'd askance, and lo! the work was done.
Was it not so with thee?
                Lut. In reason, yes;
Although I cannot answer thee in rhyme.
    VOL. IV. — 7

I saw and doubted; doubting then, I saw.
Shock'd and alarm'd, in mischief half, half fright,
I sidelong look'd as thou ——

              Isot. And saw the light.
Ha, ha! — And thus it is that men decide!
Curious to know, or vain to mark, our power,
We give some day one moment's answering look
To all the thousand we receive. At once,
Fired with the hope of conquest, the gallant,
Who never asks himself if our self-love
Or his attractions move us, lays close siege
And calls us to surrender. Yet men say,
We are the vainer!

         Lut. And I think we are.
At least they are the honester. Besiege
Or storm, their war is still in earnest. We
Fight often without object, come to terms,
Or parley but to make a safe retreat.   ,
And, if 't be gain'd by treachery, we laugh.
Isot. So will we now, and they shall be asham'd.
Help me, dear Lutia, to some rare device
Shall prove we are the better.

            Lut. First 't were well
To make sure of their purposes.

            Isot. Thou doubt'st,
Thou jealous pate! Girolamo should prefer
My livelier graces to thy sober charms,
Yet scruplest not to think those sober charms
Have caught Anselmo's fancy! Fie, oh fie!

That 's vanity, that 's prejudice, that 's to see
With purblind vision.
    Lut. Better so to see,
Than see with eyes that magnify, or give
False colors or distorted forms to things.
What can we know? This courtship of the eyes
May be but idleness, caprice at most,
Or masculine vanity: perhaps to try
Our virtue. 'T is so very odd that both
Should at one time conceive the same designs!
Isot. But quite as odd at least, that two sworn foes
Should league together to try each other's wives.
And that each for his separate self should tempt
His enemy's but to ascertain her worth —
Poh! that 's too generous: Cato's days are past,
Though borrowing wives is full as rife as ever.
As for mere vanity, or idle whim,
We soon shall see that. Wilt thou give them play?
Lut. Encourage them? Fie, Isotta!
       Isot. Wherefore, fie?
Is not Anselmo dear to me, as is
Girolamo to thee? Or deem'st thou haply,
I have designs? I were more secret then.
Lut. No, no, that is nonsense! I but mean
We stain our reputations, seeming even
To countenance their folly. I regret
To have gone so far as now.
    Isot. So do not I!
How should we find them out? And that we will;

And make them blush in the bargain.

                             Lut. At the cost
Of our own deeper blushes, and the risk
Of terrible results.

                   Isot. Now that *is* nonsense.
Why, silly child! is not our secret one?
And will not the disclosure be? The most
To dread is our lords' anger. That we 'll risk.
The game is worth it. Who shall say? perhaps
Our plot may end with making two sworn foes
Fast friends.

          Lut. Ah, might that be!

                        Isot. If then
'T were Christian to effect it, 't is our part
As Christians to attempt it.

                 Lut. Reason good,
But not the true one.

               Isot. Not for me. I own
I am just so naughty — mind thou, nothing more!
To like this mischief for itself.' 'T will be
The rarest fishing! thou with thy soft looks
To hook the mullet Barbadico, I
With craftier angling catch that nimble trout
Girolamo.

         Lut. And when they 're brought to land?

Isot. Why then — we 'll roast them.

                Lut. 'Faith, there 'll be a stew!

Isot. Go get thy lines in order.

                  Lut. What to do?

Isot. Do even as Nature prompts thee: need'st thou ask?
But let us join our maidens in the work.

Lut. Gladly; 't will be new evidence.

                              Isot. [looking off the scene to
                                        the right.

                        But see!

The signal waves. My bear is coming home.

                    [*Embracing, helps Lut. over the hedge.*

Remember now, be bold. We 'll try whose spouse
Will make the best gallant.

                        Lut. I 'll wager, mine.

Isot. I, mine, so thou wilt lure him. Ply thine eyes,
In street or room, in playhouse or at mass. [*Lutia*
                        going; Isot., also going on her side,
                                shaking her fist.

O signor mine! I 'll make thee such an ass!

                                        [*Exeunt.*

SCENE II.

The Piazzetta, or smaller Square of St. Mark.

On one side, the Ducal Palace, with the Church of St. Mark adjoining. On the other the " Procuratie" (official apartments of the " Procurators of St. Mark "). Opposite the Church, the Bell-Tower. In the background are seen the two Columns, with their statues, one of St. Mark, the other of St. Theodore. — Near the columns a group of women. Persons of various classes are walking about. And on the " Broglio" (noblemen's walk on the Palace side of the Square) are distinguished, by their sable gowns, the nobles.

Enter

ISOTTA, *with* CASSANDRA *behind her,*
the latter carrying a missal.

Then,
at a little distance, following them,
GIROLAMO.

As they cross the stage, ISOTTA *looks back over her shoulder invitingly on* GIROLAMO, *then Exit with* CASSANDRA *at the left.* GIROLAMO *comes forward.*

Girol. Eh, eh! the fruit is ripening fast. Methinks
'T will need but little shaking. Now, the maid
Leer'd on me too, with most significant eye.

Is *she* the guardian of thy orchard-wall,
Messer Anselmo, I am apt to climb. —
What if I follow, and invite the girl
By signs to parley?   If the lure succeed,
'T is well.   If not, I can but cast again.

[*Exit after them.*

Enter ANSELMO.

He holds a small and tightly folded note.

Ansel. Madonna Lutia, either thou art false
And a fit partner of thy flippant spouse,
Or thou respondest to my passionate love.
Thy soul should be the mate of mine: thy mien
Tokens deep thought, and on thy pensive brow
Is no coquetry.   Have I won thy heart? —
Shouldst thou betray me; read my written vows,
As women will do, to thy jeering friends!
The sword of my hereditary foe,
That were a trifle; but to face the laugh,
The scorn perhaps, of half of Venice, who
Would deem my passion a dishonest plot
Against my enemy's peace!   Were better death. —
But is there danger?   Here is writ no name,
Neither her own nor mine?   What could she prove?
Given in her hand at this convenient hour,
By one of those she-Mercuries [*looking up the scene,*
                    on the group near the column.
                        whose post

Is here in public and who know me not,
'T is hers or not, just as she lists; but not,
She cannot charge the missive unto me.
Hark thou, old woman! [*beckoning to one of the group.*
        But, before he can repeat the call, or has
        attracted notice,

        Enter, from the left;

        LUTIA *with* GIOVANNA.

        Heaven! here 's Lutia's self!
LUTIA *crosses the stage close before him, looking*
sidelong but demurely at him, and, just as she passes
him, drops her handkerchief. ANSELMO *picks it in-*
stantly up, folds the note in it, and hands it to her. As she
returns his bows, and curtsies her acknowledgment, LUTIA
shows consciousness and embarrassment. Exit with
        GIOVANNA, *at the right.*
'T is done now — as I did not think to do it.
But so 't is better, though undesign'd. That blush!
That conscious look! Ah here is no betrayal;
No treachery lurks beneath those drooping lids! —
Was not that handkerchief dropp'd on purpose too,
That I might speak or touch her hand? — Girolamo,
Thou 'lt pay my grandsire's dues against thy House!
But in a coin thou wilt not care to count. —
What shall I do, to master this wild joy?
'T will make a fool of me. — I'll take my gondola,
And rove about until my blood is cool. ·

*Pausing a moment, to look in the
direction which* LUTIA *had taken, he goes up the stage, passes
through the groups, and Exit.*

Re-enter, from the left, CASSANDRA
followed by GIROLAMO.

*She looks half-round, coquettishly, upon him,
as her mistress had done.* GIROLAMO *stops her, and leads
her forward.*

Girol. A word, my pretty damsel.   What 's thy name?
                         [*chucking her under the chin.*
Cass.   Cassandra, Excellence.
                         Girol. Cassandra?   Not,
I hope, a prophetess of ill to me?
Cass.   Ill?   O, I wish you all the good, I 'm sure,
That — somebody I wot of wishes you.
Girol. That somebody is not thy master.
                         Cass. No :
Not he indeed!   Now, should I like to tell
Who 't is.   But you would tell it, too.
                         Girol. Who? I?
Not I, child!   There. [*kissing her.*
                         Now, if I tell, thou canst
Tell that of me.
                         Cass. O fie! in the open Square!
A gentleman — an humble girl like me!
                         Girol. Who sees?
                         [*looking up the stage.*
Or who would mind it, if he did?   The world
    7*

Is much too busy with its own intrigues.
Come ; who is my well-wisher ?

       Cass. You 'll keep faith ?

Girol. Have I not given you pledge ?

       Cass. Well, do 't again,

Lest you forget it. [*Girol. — first looking up the stage*
       — kisses her again.

    Girol. What a jade it is !
If like the maid the mistress, as they say,
I have been belike too modest.

       Cass. That she 's not.
She would not let you kiss her in the street.

Girol. In the house, then. But, prithee, what 's her name ?
Is it thy mistress then that means me well ?

Cass. What 's she you look'd on amorously but now,
She I attended from St. Fantin's church ?

Girol. The Ser Anselmo Barbadico's spouse.

Cass. Daughter of Messer Marco Gradenigo,
Late Procurator of St. Mark, and nam'd
Isotta.

Girol. Even so much I knew.

      Cass. Is she
Worthy a gallant gentleman's devoir ?

Girol. Worthy ! Where is her equal, far or near ?

Cass. Is not Madonna Lutia fairer ?

       Girol. Come !
I want no sermons, though thou 'rt fresh from church.
I do adore thy lady.

    Cass. And she, you.

Girol. My dear Cassandra! [*hugging her.*

     Cass. Keep away! Am I

My lady's rival? And think where we are.

Now, you must know when late you pass'd us by,

Madonna said, "Cassandra, there 's a leg!"

Girol. Thou liest, thou little rogue!

       Cass. I did not say,

She said, "Behold a good one!" nor, "a stout."

She simply cried, "A leg." She saw the heel:

The rest was hidden in your sable gown.

Girol. I swear I 'll beat thee, Cassy!³

       Cass. Will you now?

Then I am off. What did you stop me for?

       [*affecting to go.*

Girol. I 'll tell thee presently. [*takes out his purse.*

     See thou here. [*opening it.*

       Cass. Oh stay,

There 's something more, though not about the leg.

One day, when you were standing by your door,

Caressing a small dog, my lady said,

Sighing, "I would I were that little cur!" —

"Madonna, why?"— "Because"— she sigh'd

 again —

"The Ser Girolamo has so white a hand."

Girol. Say'st thou, my mocking waiting-woman? Well,

Let thy mirth pay thee. [*affecting to put back his

        purse.*

   Thou 'rt a little fool.

Cass. I were, to let you go away displeas'd.

A hand and leg are really no mean parts.
Yet not for those alone my lady loves you.
Girol. Canst thou be serious for one moment?

        Cass. Two.

What does your Excellence command?

       Girol. Take this.

        [*giving her a ducat of gold.*

Cass. Is it for me, or for my mistress?

       Girol. Pish!

Here is another piece of gold. Wilt thou
Bear me a message to thy lady's ear?
Cass. O yes, I 'll tell her that you doat on legs,
And wish you were the mass-book in her hands.
Girol. Hark thou, fair Trojan! I am mirthful too;
But there 's a time for all things. See thou then,
We shall be noted, standing here so long.
Cass. And what too, should my master come this way!

      [*draws her scarf over her head.*

Girol. [*his hand upon her arm.*

  Come then, if thou wilt prate, beneath the arches;
Or, follow me to my gondola.

       Cass. No, no.

Be brief; and pardon me. I did impose
On your good temper.

      Girol. Wilt thou bear my word?
Cass. I will, and truly.

      Girol. But how do I know
Thy lady is not mocking me through thee?
Cass. By your own eyes, which must have seen ere this

What passes in Madonna's heart; and by
Your consciousness that as you are not pleas'd
With Monna Lutia, so Messer' Anselmo
May be too owlish for my lady's taste.
Like pairs with like: and yo aro like.

       Girol. Well said.
Thou art a cuuning giglet.   Plead my cause.
There is thy fee.   If thou shouldst gain my suit,
Thou hast the triple of it.

    Cass. What to sue ?
Girol. Sue for an hour's meeting.   Where and when
I leave to her own gracious will.

       Cass. How sue ?
Girol. Sue by my passion; sue by her own charms ;
Ask in thy own heart — 't is a woman's ; there
Are all thy law-books, — and thou hast thy brief.
Go, pretty advocate, and bring me fortune.

Cass. You are a gallant gentleman.   I would,
In sooth I would, it were another suit
Than to your neighbor's wife.

       Girol. Thou 'rt not to preach.
The worse my cause, the better shalt thou plead.
Paint what I feel ; thou canst not paint too warmly :
Say what thou seest; but see with kindly eyes. •

Cass.   And shall I tell her all?

      Girol. Tell all — but this.

         [kissing her.

Cass. [*extricates herself with a laugh, then, shaking her
  finger at him.*

Nay, I 'll tell all; it were a sin to miss.
A leg! a hand! and O ma'am, such a kiss!

                [Exit Cass. at the left.

GIROLAMO *looking after her a moment,*
half in vexation, half in satisfaction, goes up the stage to
mingle with the nobles on the Broglio, and
Scene closes.

SCENE III.

The Garden — as in Scene I.

ISOTTA.   LUTIA.   GIOVANNA.

Isot. [*looking up from a letter she has been reading.*
    So far, thou hast won the wager. Who 'd have
      thought
    The dignified Anselmo was so sly?
    So boldly gallant too! and so adroit!
Lut. 'T was featly done. He must have had good practice.
Isot. Ay, but the kerchief was as nicely dropp'd.
    I must be cautious: thou art stately too.
Lut. Fie now, Isotta! Jealous?

                Isot. Jealous? Hum!

'T is the scant brook that bubbles o'er the stones;
Deep lakes are placid.
           Lut. Always?   Now, methinks,
Rough waters do most mischief.
                 Isot. Let us see. [*affecting*
                    anxiously to read the letter.
Here are a dozen fires, and pains, and faiths:
O sanctity!   And here —— Why here, he boasts
Of favoring looks!
            Lut. I never gave but one —
Always except this last, which was agreed.
And then the note was written.
                 Isot. Mere evasion!
Would he have ventur'd else? so proud? so shy?
Thou art the lake.   Thy depths shall not ingulf
My treasure, my lord's love.
               Lut. Isotta dear!
Isot. Thou shalt not grant this meeting which he prays:
I will not trust thee.
            Lut. Thou shalt have no need.
'T was not my project; and I like it not.
But seems it ——
            Isot. Peace! I will have my revenge.

Enter CASSANDRA, *in great glee.*

Now comes my turn. —
           Lut. Giovanna, to the house,
And watch for both. [*Exit, over the hedge, Giovanna.*

Isot. Well! Hast thou lur'd the hawk?
Did the trout nibble? Is the leopard snar'd?
Cass. See here! [*holding up the two gold pieces.*
And here — and here — and here:
[*touching her lips with her hand three times.*
And here again! [*puts her arm around her own waist*
caressingly.

Isot. Three kisses, and a hug!
Why here's a brave gallant! What say'st thou now?
[*to Lut.*
Thy man is worse than mine! [*Lutia has turn'd away.*
Why, Lutia dear,
Thou art not crying? Couldst thou think indeed,
That I was jealous? Jealous? Jealous, I?
And jealous too of thee? My own dear girl,
My sister! Thou shalt have Anselmo all,
And keep Girolamo too. Now, do but laugh!
Lut. How can I laugh to know my lord so vile?
Isot. Vile? Art thou crazy? He is but a man;
Girolamo Bembo, not Girolamo Saint.
Why what a child thou beest! I'll wager now
My wedding-robes against thy bedroom-gown,
This wanton tempted him. Come, didst thou not?
Cass. Only one kiss. The rest were volunteer'd.
The hug was all his own.
Isot. [*laughing heartily, while Lutia*
smiles.

Eh, Lutia, see!
This jolly wight was surely meant for me.

How wilt thou change him for my sober lord?

Lut. [*to Cass.*

But what was all this for?

     Cass. This what, Madonna?

This kissing? or this hugging? In good sooth,

I think he took me for my lady here.

Isot. Out, baggage! Am I such a colt as thou?

Cass. I cannot tell, Madonna; but he said,

He had been too modest, — mistress like, like maid.

Lut. There now, Isotta!

    Isot. 'T is her wanton pranks.

Thou hast overdone thy part, thou naughty jade!

What didst thou tell him?

    Cass. That you prais'd his leg —

Although you never saw it.

     Lut. Brava! } *nearly*

     Isot. Heigh! } *together.*

Cass. And seeing his white hand on a greyhound lie,

You wish'd yourself the puppy for its sake.

Isot. I vow I'll beat thee!

    Cass. So he threaten'd too.

You are so alike!   '

    Isot. I 'll pinch thee black and blue!

Thou hast marr'd our acting.

    Cass. No, I mind my cue.

I made him think you so ador'd his face,

He fairly hugg'd me — in the public place!

Lut. Thou hast taught her well — thy rhyming too, I see.

Isot. But never mind; the hug was not for thee. —

And finally, what bring'st thou from my swain? .

Cass. These golden ducats.

                 Isot. They 're for thee, not me.

Cass. To plead his passion.

                 Isot. A retaining-fee.

Cass. The suit once won, my client makes the twain
A pair of triplets.

             Isot. Briefly, what to gain?
Thou keep'st Madonna Lutia in her pain.

Cass. Messer Girolamo bids me thus to sue.
By his own passion, by his lady's charms —
That is not Monna Lutia's? — you would grant
Your knight an interview; the when and where,
That leaves he safely to your modest self

Isot. Ha, ha! 'T is done! We 're quits: the game is
    square.
Thy note is match'd. Was ever such a pair!

Lut. Nay, thy Anselmo was the first to woo.

Isot. But thy Girolamo has courted two.
His suit takes time: too fiery to be stay'd,
He tries his mettle on my waiting-maid!

Cass. Perhaps 'twas offer'd as a sample-bliss:
I told him I should recommend his kiss.

Lut. Now what 's to do?

             Isot. Is that a point to moot?
Do as kind ladies, grant to each his suit.
Now, shut that little mouth! [*putting her hand on
                  Lutia's lips.*

           I 'll not hear nay.

We 'll meet the pair.

     Lut. But not in their own way?

Isot. No, plan we both; thou in thy closet, sweet,

And I in mine.

     Lut. To plot, when next we meet.

Isot. Adieu! Take this — and this — and this: [*kissing*

           her three times.

            this too.

           [*hugging her.*

Cassandra brought them.

     Lut. But to give to you.

Isot. I wave my right.

     Lut. [*kissing her in turn.*

    Nay, keep them: they 're thy due.

      [*Goes over the hedge.*

Isot. How is 't, Cassandra?

     Cass. I no difference see:

Ye have the shells; the oyster rests with me.

Lut. [*from over the hedge, and going.*

  Adieu, Isotta!

     Isot. 'Drina,* let us flee.

       [*Exeunt omnes.*

ACT THE SECOND

SCENE I. *A room in the house of Giovanni Moro.*

MORO. GISMONDA.

Moro. It boots not to remonstrate; I am fix'd:
   The Doge's nephew shall not enter here.
Gism. Poor Aloise! I have heard thee say,
   Father, he was a brave and noble youth.
Moro. Thou may'st again, if that will do thee good.
   The son of Marco Foscari, men report,
   Is a magnanimous and right valiant soul,
   Though rash and over-ardent: faults perhaps
   These of his yet young blood. I grant him too
   One quality more, appropriate to his rank,
   That thy late husband wanted. He is rich;
   At least will be, when Marco sleeps with Mark.
   Poor Niccolò Delfino, though a brave   .
   Good husband and right worshipful cavalier,
   Left thee scant store of zecchins. 'T was thy choice.
   I have not repented *then* I gave thee way.'
   But *now* I will not.
                    Gism. Yet, dear father, hear! ——
Moro. Not a word more! Must I repeat, Gismonda,
   That with the hated blood of Francis Foscari
   No drop of Loredano's ever mingles?

Gism. Ours is so small a drop! We are but cousins,
Four times remov'd. And thou hat'st not the Foscari.

Moro. No, but I am the Admiral Pietro's friend.
He scorn'd the Doge's daughter for his son :
I cannot give the nephew of the Doge
My only child; and for a twofold cause.
First, I should rouse dark Loredano's hate;
A fearful man! that never yet forgave;
Then Marco Foscari's, who has promis'd, thou know'st,
His son to Lisa, daughter of his friend,
The rich Avvogadórè, Morosini.

Gism. Alas!

Moro. Alas? Alas for me, thou meanest.
Should I not waken too the Doge's ire?
Blunt though I be, I want no man's ill will,
Though I court no man's favor.

                    Gism. But these feuds!
Father, there are our neighbors, the Messeri
Bembo and Barbadico : who can hate
More cordially than they? whose sires, they tell,
Even in Doge Soranza's time — that 's now
More than a hundred years — were foes. Yet see!
They married foster-sisters and warm friends,
Who for their sakes meet never, save abroad.

Moro. What 's that to Marco Foscari's son and thee?
His sire is not consenting as theirs were.
I have no feud with Foscari. But I say —
A plague upon thy womans-cares! I say —
I say, I 'll not wake Loredano's spite.

Let the Duke's nephew carry his pretensions
To Lisa; this is interdicted ground,
Like Bembo's house to Barbadico's spouse.

Gism. Poor Aloise! his impassion'd soul ——

Moro. Impassion'd pudding! What 's his soul to me?[6]
Go get thee a new lover; men are cheap.

Gism. I had not thought to hear this from those lips.
Men cheap, my father? Is it then of men
Like Aloise Foscari thou speakest?
Brave as his warlike uncle, generous, just,
Sagacious, resolute, where wilt thou find
More honor for our House, a stouter prop
For thy declining years, a nobler hope
For thy large heritage through thy only child,
Than the Duke's nephew, Marco Foscari's heir?
As lofty a spirit as ever grac'd a throne![7]

Moro. Were it the Duke himself, I might relent,
But being his nephew only, I will not.[6]
As for the honor, Foscari is no more
Than Moro; for my years, as yet, thank God!
They are not much o'er the hill-top; when declining
Into the vale, I 'll hear thee talk of props.
And for my heritage, 't is no fault of mine
Thy bed is yet a widow's. Make thy choice.
So he be not a citizen or tradesman,
Gambler or brawler, drunkard or a thief,
John Moro will not say Gismonda nay.[9]

Gism. My choice is made: I cannot change it, father.
My faith is given: thou wouldst not have it broke?

Moro. Then so are mine.   And this is choice and faith :
Let Foscari be thy lover, an' thou will;
But it shall not be in thy father's house.
Thou hast been wedded; thou canst make thy home
Even where thou wilt.   But let thy scanty means
Furnish thy narrow household.   By St. John !
I will not give one zecchin in thy aid !
Gism. O be not so obdurate !
                         Moro. Not one zecchin !
If Marco to his disobedient son
Will prove more kind, I wish thee joy of it. [*Going.*
Gism. Be not so angry, dear my father ! ——
        Moro. [*breaking from her ; but coldly.*] Peace !
Gism. If Aloise ——
            Moro. Be a fool, must thou ?
Thou hast heard my reasons, and thou knowest my
    will.
Do thy own pleasure.   But of this rest sure :
If Procurator Marco's son come in,
Messer Delfino's widow shall go out.[10] [*Exit.*
Gism. And I might find it in my heart to do so,
Thou art so unsympathetic, and so harsh.
But thou wouldst then be childless and alone.
Childless alone !   Heaven pardon me the thought !
'T was sinful-selfish.   And then Aloise !
To involve him in distress !—   But what to do ?
It is his hour ! —
Goes hastily to a door in the back of the scene, and opens it,
            displaying a corridor.

What, Giulietta![11] [*clapping her hands.*

Quick! —

If they should meet!   My father's sullen mien —
And *his* quick temper!—

Enter, through the door,

GIULIETTA.

To the basement!   haste!

Is Messer Aloise landed, lead him
Somewhere away, and tell him this from me:
My sire has knowledge of his visits here
And will not longer bear them.   Does he love me,
He will not press to come — not now; my father
Is sullen, when oppos'd. — If not yet come,
Wait thou his gondola, and wave him off
To the next Canal.   There haste to meet him.   Go.
Bid him have patience.

[*Exit Giulietta.*

Patience?   And I need

So much myself!   I made so sure to-day
That I should see him!   I so little thought
My father would be adverse! —   Aloise!
Wilt thou preserve unstain'd thy maiden faith? —
Between two hostile influences; and the charms
Of Lisa Morosini —— O my heart!
The sacrifice which threatens will prove hard. —
If Aloise tempt me to rebel ——
My lonely sire!   Again that selfish thought.
I must not think it.   Yet these senseless feuds!

What are their hates to us ?   If Marco Foscari,
Who dotes upon his gallant son, give way,
(My sire is rich as Lisa's, — may he not ?)
And move my colder father !   O dear hope !
Let me not lose thee !   Though it rain to-day,
The sun shines out to-morrow.   Then comes peace —
Oomes father's blessing — comes joy — comes Aloise !
                                              [*Exit.*

SCENE II.

The Piazetta — as in Act I. Sc. II.

In the background, scattered groups and promenaders.

After some moments,

Enter, from the side, GIULIETTA,

followed by ALOISE.

She comes forward, stops, and awaits him.

Alo. What is it, girl ?   How fares thy lady ?   Speak ?
Giul. Well, Messer Aloise ; well, but vex'd.
     VOL. IV.—8

His Excellence, my master, — who, be 't said
Between us, is the crossest crab alive —
Always sour and sullen, as if he meant to snap,
Like the old crocodile on the pillar-top
Of San Teodoro yonder ——

                  Alo. Well, well, well!

Giul. Has been I suppose in such an ugly mood,
   Madonna bade me haste to you, to say
   You are not to come to the palace any more;
   His Excellence has found you out.—

                  Alo. Me out?

Giul. Both of you-out: which is a burning shame;
   I made so sure your Excellence and she
   Would one of these days be fix'd together fast,
   Like Adam and Eve at Marco's corner yon.

Alo. Art thou quite sure?

              Giul. As I am standing here.
   I know it because she bade you patience have.
   She had not done this, had she not made sure
   You 'd not have any.

             Alo. O Giulietta dear!
   To-day I was to have seen her.   'T is so long
   Since I have heard her speak, except to say
   Good-morrow, or Good-even!   Canst thou not
   Admit me for a little while, — by stealth,
   If so it must be?

            Giul. Now? Messerè, no.
   The master is at home.   And so my lady
   Bids you take note, "he is sullen if oppos'd."

Which means you must, I take it, for her sake,
Not put your fingers in the old crab's claws.
"Does he love me, he will not press," she said,
"Not now, to come."

     Alo. I will not then, not now.
But now is not forever.   When her sire
Is no more at the house, then may I come.
Go back and tell her, Giuliet, I will wait—
Until she hang some signal — say, a glove,
Out at her window.   Never shake thy head.
Who shall know aught of it ?   Is the Casa Mora
Not built like other noble houses here ?
The women's rooms are in the hinder part,
Divided from the men's ?[12]   Is not that so ?

Giul. Happily so.   A wise provision, where
Such gruff old lords as Messer Moro rule.
Unhappily though, or happily, for you,
Just as you rate Madonna, she is built
Unlike some other noble ladies here,
At least in the inside.   She will not consent
To have you come to the hinder part of the house.

Alo. I did not mean it, girl.   I but beseech her
To make some sign when she shall be prepar'd
To admit me as before.

     Giul. That cannot be ;
Not till this storm, whate'er it be, is over.
When sudden winds sweep over the Lagune,
Your gondoliers make instantly for the shore,
And wait till the flurry is spent.   So must you do,

Or look to get a ducking, or be drown'd.
Monna Gismonda begs you will have patience.
When it 's fair weather, Messer Aloise,
You can put out again.
               Alo. But until then !
But until then !   Think of my torments, girl !
And think of hers !   Have pity on us both !
I have so much to say !   I cannot rest
Until I know what this new trouble is.
  And she, how she must long to tell me !   Go !
Go, tell her that I must, I must, will see her !
Go, for thy lady's sake, if not for mine !
Giul. How does your Excellence know Madonna suffers ?
Alo. By my own feeling.   If she do not long,
And in her longing suffer, as I do ;
 If she would not give up a week of life
For one hour's talk with me, as I would gladly,
O a whole twelvemonth ! for an hour with her.
Then will I beg no more ; she is unworthy
Of love like mine.
           Giul. She is not ! not unworthy ! —
Now, do not stop this little brain of mine ;
I am contriving. — Let me see. — I have it !
How will the night do ?   Could you talk in the dark,
In the open air, as well as in a room ?
Alo. Dear Giulietta !   Giuliettina !   Speak !
                    [*taking her hands.*
Giul. Pray, don't make love to me.   Now, do keep still !
 'T is not in the dark here, tho' it 's open enough.

And I am not Madonna. Since you know
So well the woman's side of the house, you know
There are balcónies[12] on the second floor
To all the windows. Could your Excellence climb
To the large middle one ? 'T is not a steep
So easy as the Bell-Tower ; nor the view
Quite so extensive ; but you 'll like it better.
Alo.   You are an angel ! [*about to hug her.*

     Giul. Now, now, do forbear !
I am ticklish. — Well, what will your Excellence do ?
And what shall I ?

    Alo. Do ? do ? Go back at once.
Say to Madonna, will she please let down ——
At what hour were it best ?

     Giul. About the fourth.
'T will then be midnight, and the Cà[14] Veniero
Will like our own be quiet.

     Alo. — Will she please
With her fair hands let down ——

     Giul. Or better, 'mine,
Which are not fair ——

    Alo. Peace, saucy one ! — Let down
From the mid window, when St. Mark tolls four,[16]
A length of cord, I will make fast thereto
A hempen ladder.

    Giul. Which we two draw up
With our four hands, and fasten to the rails.
Well, Messer Aloise ; but ill-reckon'd.
There is this to add to the account : Madonna

May not consent.

    Alo. How canst thou be so cruel?
Hast thou not words? and canst thou not persuade?
Thou knowest her humor well. But tell her this —
And it is solemn truth; I shall not rest
Until I see her; care will murder sleep.
Tell her, O tell her, all that thou canst think,
All thy own heart may teach, to move her pity.
Thou canst not say too much, or make my love
More than it is, my suffering than 't will be.
Take thou this ring, Giulietta. 'T is a ruby
Of no mean value. Wear it for my sake,
An earnest of the good I mean to do thee,
Wilt thou be kind.

    Giul. No, Messer Aloise.
You are a generous young lord, I see,
As men report you, and Madonna thinks.
But keep the ring. I need it not from you.
When you are wedded to Madonna Mora,
Then will I take your presents. Now, farewell.
If I can win Madonna to consent,
She will to-night admit you, it may be
Even to her chambers, since I shall be there.

Alo. Dear Giulietta!

    Giul. Not yet; not so fast.
St. Geminy! Take heed! if not more slow
To-night in climbing, you may get a fall. —
Once more: — In half an hour, pass you the house.
If I have won Madonna to your suit,

You will see a red string hanging from the casement.
'T is there, at that balcony, you will mount. [*going.*
Alo. Giulietta! Giuliettina! Stop, awhile.
Thou art a precious maiden. When I make
Monna Gismonda mine, then will I find thee
A brave young husband for thyself.

       Giul. Like you?
Thank you, Messerè. Such a one shall need
No ladder to climb up to me. Farewell. [*going.*
Alo. 'T is thou art hasty, now. Thou hast not heard all.
To-night I'll fling a pebble at the casement,
When the bell tolls; so will she know 't is I.
Giul. You are then quite sure Madonna is to yield?
Alo. Sure in your dextrous handling.

      Giul. Right! How else?
I have two men to throw for: you for her,
And a brave husband like yourself for me. .

         [*Exit.*
ALOISE *stands still a moment, looks about him,*
   then slowly follows her.

SCENE III.

The Apartment of Gismonda.

*A room having a large casement-window, extending to the
floor, and opening on a balcony.*

GISMONDA

walking impatiently about.

Gism. What can detain her?   What is there to say?
 He is filling now her happy ears with words —
 Words of deep love and passionate prayer — for me:
 He is teaching her persuade me ——
                    listening.] Was that she?
 No; 't was the sea-breeze playing through the blinds. —
 He is teaching her to move me to have pity.
 Ah, Aloise! Aloise! here,
 Here, here already, all the words of love
 That thou canst send me, in my brain are stirring:
 The heart inspires them fast as thou canst speak;
 They plead as warmly for thee, as thy words,
 Even could I hear thy own lips utter them,
 Could plead for thee; they plead to my own heart,
 Coming from my heart, and plead too for my heart.
 O in this void that is such pleasing pain,
 This thrilling of the pulse ——
                    starting.] That! that is she!

Runs eagerly to the side scene

as Enter GIULIETTA.

GISMONDA *draws her eagerly forward.*

At last! at last!   I thought that thou wast dead.

Giul. I am almost dead with running — up the staircase.

Gism.. What said he?   What said Messer Aloise?

Giul. What did he?   What did Messer Aloise?

O he 's a rare gallant!

        Gism. Quick! Giulietta!

What said he?

      Giul. Messer Niccolò Delfino——

Gism. Leave Messer Niccolò Delfino bury'd.

Giul. With all my heart.   He has been two years fast

    sleeping;

I do not wish to wake him.   He was but

A log to your new husband, that will be.

Gism. Why, what means this?   What 's got into the girl?

Giul. Pure love and admiration.   Such a noble!

He tried to hug me.

       Gism. I am much oblig'd to him.

Giul. He call'd me Angel.

       Gism. It was very kind.

Giul. [*laughing.*

Now don't, now don't be jealous, dear Madonna!

'T was all on your account.

       Gism. I do not like

Such gifts by proxy.

       Giul. No, our natural wants

8*

Are best serv'd by ourselves.   So I refus'd
To taste for you, Madonna.

     Gism. Giulïetta!

This is a style ——

    Giul. Now do not be displeas'd!
I really think, Madonna, for your sake,
I am more than over head and ears in love
With Messer Aloise: and I promis'd ——

Gism. Well, well, Giulietta, tell me thine own way,
 Since thou wilt not in mine.   But prithee, child,
 Why twin'st thou that red ribbon round thy fingers?

Giul. It is my garter, Madam, which I dropp'd
 In coming up the stair.   I would not then
 Take time to put it on.

    Gism. Well, put it by. [*Giul. puts the*
        string into her bosom.

Now say, what said he?

    Giul. All that man could say.
He had made so sure to see you! [*Gism. sighs.*

       't was so long
Since he had seen you! he should never rest
Till he should see you! he was so perplex'd
He could not see you! he so long'd to hear
Why now he could not see you!   And, in short,
Distress'd, bewilder'd, full of love and pity,
I promis'd him ——

    Gism. Ha! what?

     Giul. That you would see him.

Gism. Thou art the sauciest ——

Giul. Best-disposed poor creature.
Pardon me I dare interrupt, Madonna!
But had you seen him — [*Gism. sighs again.*
                    heard him, — as I saw,
And heard him, you yourself, in love and pity,
Had promis'd too.
                    Gism. I had not needed then,
Had I so seen and heard him.   Thou dost jest,
Or thou art impudent, with thy love and pity.
Giul. All for your sake, Madonna.
                    Gism. For mine too,
Thou promis'dst he should see me?
                    Giul. No, for both.
Gism. How now!   Or Messer Aloise Foscaro
Has with my maid forgot himself and me,
Or thou 'rt beside thyself.   What has he done,
Or said, to make thee so presumptuous?   Has
He given thee aught?
                    Giul. He offer'd me a ring.
I would not take it.
                    Gism. He has promis'd then ——
Giul. Only a husband.
                    Gism. Thou art malapert!
And when I am so vex'd, too!   Get thee hence.
Giul. No, let me stay, Madonna.   Why be vex'd
That I am merry, when I am but so
Only because I thought to make you happy,
And make him happy, who deserves to be?
Will you not hear me?

Gism. Speak then, as thou should'st.
Speak plainly, in few words. What didst thou promise?
Giul. Nothing, Madonna: only that I would
Try to persuade you to admit him here,
To-night.

     Gism. Here, in my chamber? Didst thou dare
To so disgrace me? Get thee to him back,
And say, thou hast mista'en me. Go at once!
Giul. O madam! do but hear me! do not be
So wroth with my well-meaning! I will beg,
If so it must be, on my knees for pardon,
If I have done you wrong. But only hear me!
What was there so amiss in what I said?
Here was the Doge's nephew so distress'd
It would have mov'd Mark's lion, or my master,
Praying an humble girl like me to have
Compassion on him?

         Gism. Was he so distress'd?
Giul. In sooth, Madonna, how could he be else,
So loving you, and of so great a heart? [*Gism. sighs.*
Just in the moment when he should be bless'd
In seeing you, to be bidden not to come.
Another man had mov'd me, so perplex'd;
But he so noble, such a god in mien!
Gism. [*sighing again.*

     Indeed, I was most sorry. 'T was with pain
Unto myself. But what was to be done?
Didst not thou, dear Giulietta, tell him all?
How sullen was my father?

Giul. All.   I said,
He was a crab, a crooodile — St. Teddy's[18]
Old crocodile on the pillar.
                    Gism. Thou shouldst not
Have us'd such phrases.
                    Giul. Could I pick my words?
I was so vex'd.   And there was Messer Foscaro,
Begging, with his sweet voice, as if he were
An orphan whose last parent had been drown'd
In the Canal by order of the Ten,
That I would have some little pity on him,
And let him in by stealth : it was so long
Since he had heard you speak, except to say,
Good-morrow, or Good-even. [*Gism. turns her head*
                    away abruptly.
                    O Madonna,
It makes me weep to only tell his words;
As it does you, I think, to hear them told.
Gism. [*in a soft and broken voice.*
    No matter, dear Giulietta: say some more.
Giul. I bade him to be patient, as you said,
    But as he was beside himself with grief,
    And fear of something wrong, and talk'd of care,
    And murdering sleep, and other horrid things,
    I thought to soothe him by a gentle hint,
    Perhaps you would — now don't be wroth, Madonna!
    See him awhile by night, since I should be
    Along with you the while, and you might talk
    In the balcony, in the open air.

Gism. 'T was very wrong. [*faintly.*

> *Giul.* I did but hint, Madonna.
> I promis'd nought ; I said that I would try.
> I will go back, and tell him not to come.

Gism. No, be not hasty.   Seem'd he much distress'd ?

Giul. Ask your own heart, Madonna ; as he said,
> I must my own to tell me what he felt ;
> Which was quite handsome in him.   For your sake,
> He said, I must persuade you, as for his.

Gism. Did he ? [*sharply.*

> *Giul.* I ask'd him how he knew you suffer'd.
> He said — so proudly ! with such passion too !
> It really made my heart go pit-a-pat :
> " By my own feeling.   If she do not long,
> And in her longing suffer, as I do ;
> If she would not give up a week of life
> For one hour's talk with me, as I would gladly,
> O a whole twelvemonth, for an hour with her ;
> Then will I beg no more : she is unworthy
> Of love like mine ! "

> > *Gism.* I am not ! not unworthy !

Giul. And so I said ; and in those very words !
> Now, dear Madonna, do consent !   How can you
> At once so feel, and not feel ?

> > *Gism.* Give me time.

GISMONDA *turning away,*
and standing pensive, her back to the window and her head
down, GIULIETTA *seizes the opportunity,*
and, taking the ribbon

from her bosom, trips to the window,
pushes open the casement, goes on the balcony,
and is seen to fasten the ribbon to the balustrade. As she
is about to close the casement again,
GISMONDA *turns.*

Gism. What mak'st thou out at the window, Giulïetta ?

Giul. To see if Messer Foscari were there.

Gism. And was he ? [*eagerly.*

    Giul. Yes.

        Gism. Let me see too.

            Giul. Now nay,

                [*intercepting her.*

He is no longer; and the Cà Veniero

Has windows too.

        Gism. Which thou hadst quite forgot.

What led thee to suppose he would be there ?

Giul. I promis'd I would give him sign of hope.

Gism. And didst thou ?

        Giul. O be not severe, Madonna !

Hope is a blessing.

        Gism. When it leads astray ?

Giul. But now it will not lead astray, Madonna.

I know it will not.   Shall I on my knees,

And pray you to be just ? or shall I weep,

And tell again his suffering ?   O Madonna !

It is so small a thing !

        Gism. For thee, not me.

Giul. But shall I not be with you all the while ?

And have you not been married ?   What he asks,

What maiden would refuse? I do not think
That Monna Lisa would.

      Gism. Stop now ; no more.
I will bethink me. Said he then, to-night?

Giul. At the fourth hour to-night. Think — 't is his
  words —
Think of his torments ; think of yours ; he has
So much to ask you ; you, so much to tell ;
Have pity then on both. I know you will.

Gism. [*going.*
    Thou know'st too much then. I will go consider.

Giul. 'T is to resolve. Else hardly would you give
Seven days of life for one hour's talk with him.

Gism. Hush, hush ! Thou know'st not.

        Giul. But I know that he
Would give a twelvemonth for an hour with you.

Gism. Hush ! [*Exit.*

    Giul. Here 's a work to meet one cavalier !
St. Moses ![17] I would meet one every night !

  Goes to the balcony, and returns with
    the ribbon.

Had she but seen my garter ! — Never mind !
Why not as well a knee-band as an armlet
To noose a husband ? If I catch one too,
(And I have earn'd him ; it has been hard work !)
I 'll strip the other off, and make the set
A votive offering to St. Giuliet.[18] [*Exit.*

Act the Third

Scene I. *The Garden — as in Act I., Sc. I.*

Enter on the upper side

Lutia *and* Giovanna.

The latter comes over the hedge, then helps

Lutia *to follow.*

Lut. Thou 'rt sure she said her master was abroad?
Giov. Madonna, yes. 'T is Holy Vito's day.¹⁹
He is at the church.
    Lut. So are we wholly free.

Enter

Isotta *and* Cassandra.

And here they come. Now shall we see.
    Isot. [*embracing her.*] See what?
Lut. This "loveliest plot that ever was devis'd."
Isot. And 't is. Had Baimont Tiepolo's been as fair,
My ducal ancestor had been put down,
And I perhaps been not put forth, to achieve
A marital reform.
    Lut. It is the day
That plot was thwarted. Omen of ill luck.

Isot. To our lords, not us. — Now hear.   To-night——
                                Lut. To-night ?

Isot. At the fourth hour ——
                        Lut. That 's midnight.
                                Isot. Even so.
— We see each other's chambers for the first,
But not I hope the last time.
                        Lut. What means that ?

Isot. It means, our lovers meet us there to-night,
And we our husbands.   Seest thou ?
                            Lut. Not a ray !

Isot. Then might'st thou carry, for all the good they do,
    Thine eyes in a platter, like thy patron-saint.
Cass. That, save the platter, were as well for both,
    Seeing both the gentlemen woo you in the dark.
Isot. Now what behold'st thou ?
                        Lut. Twilight, not full day.

Isot. Thou art but half-awake ! 'T would serve thee right,
    To let thee grope, as good Anselmo will,
    When he seeks Monna Lutia in the night,
    And finds he is saddled with Isotta still.
    Now seest thou well ? or art thou still abed ?
Lut. I see the plan.
                    Isot. And think'st of it ?
                            Lut. With dread.
'T will ruin us both.
                    Isot. Thou hast the drollest head !
Here are Giovanna and Cassandra both.
They know all, and take part in all.   Our truth

Has their assurance.

Lut. Will that stay the wrath
Of either cavalier, when found the cheat
We have put upon him? Think too of their hate
Envenom'd by the consciousness of wrong
Design'd against each other!

Isot. That I leave
To Providence, believing in my soul
Shame will extinguish wrath. But for their rage
Against our innocent selves, why let it burn!
A double storm of feminine reproach
Will blow it out, I think, and cool their brains
For just conviction. — But I do not mean
They soon shall find the cheat. Not till at least
Our double game is won. Look at our make:
We are enough alike. Then, bred together,
Our voices have one tone. We shall not speak
More than is needful.

Lut. I shall not, I am sure.
Girolamo will think it very odd
In gay Isotta.

Isot. No, he 'll deem her coy
Or prudent. Fearing no deceit, be sure
Their amorous fancies will delude them both.
But whether or not, we have ridden too far, my dear,
Now to draw bridle: win we not the race,
We are ruin'd beyond redemption.

Lut. 'T is too true.
Our lovers are grown importunate, and believe

Each that his neighbor has a shameless wife.

Isot. So let them; till we make them blush to own
They are bad husbands, we the best of wives.
And this my plan. Cassandra on my part
Shall tell Girolamo, that my lord to-night
Takes barque for Padua, and invite him come
At the fourth hour. From thee Giovanna bears
A letter to Anselmo ——

     Lut. Why a letter

From me?

   Isot. Because he wrote one unto thee.
'T will suit his gravity better.

      Lut. Well. To say?——

Isot. Girolamo at Murano with some friends
Will pass the entire night; and that between
The third and fourth hour he may venture in.

Lut. But why thus earlier?

     Isot. Out; thou silly thing!
Not that I want my spouse a half hour more;
But to prevent the two encountering. Well:
At the third hour, or even before, we enter
Each other's house, here by the garden-gate,
And by each other's maid are led straightway
Each to the other's chamber, there inspect
All that belongs to it, and when 't is known
Put out the lights, and so await ——

      Lut. In terror.

Isot. Fie, timid one! Are they not given to know
We meet in the dark, and neither is to speak?

Lut. But will it not be best to send my letter
By some hired messenger ?

       Isot. That, as thou lik'st. —
Now haste, my Lutia. [*embracing her. Then,*
    laughingly.] But restrain thy muse ;
Be not too fond! Anselmo might expect
Too much of cold Isotta.

       Lut. And yet find
More than Girolamo will in Lutia warm.

Cass. Pardon me, ladies, if I dare suggest :
Madonna Isotta should compose this letter.

Isot. As knowing her husband's solemn humor best.

Cass. No, as new proof.

       Isot. — Than one, two heads are better.
'T is well. I 'll throw it o'er the hedge. Thou, sweet,
Shall copy it and send it.

       Lut. And so fetter
These *Husband-Lovers* with a chain complete
Of evidence. My heart not now will flutter.

Isot. Hey then for frolic and our *Double* cheat!

    [*kissing Lut., — who, with Giov., Exit over*
     the hedge, while Isot. and Cass. Exeunt
     on their side.

SCENE II.

As in Scene III., Act II.

Enter

GISMONDA *and* GIULIETTA,

*the latter bearing a lighted wax-candle and a coil
of slender cord. She blows out the light;
and* GISMONDA *opens the casement.*

Gism. The crescent moon gives just sufficient light.
More would betray us.   Look down into the street.
Seest thou aught yet?
   Giul. Madonna, nothing yet.
'T is black as pitch.
    Gism. The alley is so narrow,
And we are up so high.   It will be hard,
I fear, to climb. *[anxiously.*
   Giul. Fear not: a lover's legs ——
Hark! I hear something.
    Gism. Speak more softly then:
'T may be some other.
    Giul. How fearfully you tremble!
Courage, Madonna!—Hark now!   There goes St.
 Mark!
One — two — three — four!
*As the sound of the last stroke dies away, something light is
thrown against the casement.*
    Gism. [*eagerly, but in an under tone.*

And there 's the signal-stone!
Quick, Giulietta!

GISMONDA *lets down the cord, while* GIULIETTA *holds it.*

Giul. See you yet, Madonna?

Gism. Yes, though but dimly. — Now, he shakes the cord!
Draw up.

*They pull on the cord together. The head of the ladder
becomes visible. They secure it to the balustrade.*

Giul. 'T is fasten'd now.   'T is quite secure.

Gism. He pulls upon 't to try.—   He 's on it now!—
He mounts!—He 's half-way up!—He 's ——— Aloïse!

> [*with deep tenderness, and stretching out
> her arms over the balustrade.*

Alo. [*within — as just under the balcony.*

Gismonda!

*Immediately, the ladder appears to be jerked violently; and
there is an ill-defined dull noise.*

Gism. O God! he has fallen! he is dead!

> *Giul.* Hush, hush![20]

Look, dear Madonna! he moves! he is but hurt.
He holds both hands to his head.   Your eyes now us'd
To peer in the darkness, you may see him plain.
He is going off!—   O why so still, Madonna?
You frighten me.   Do speak to me!

> *Gism.* [*who, the whole time Giul. has been speak-
> ing in a suppressed voice, has been lean-
> ing over the balustrade, now looking
> up, and in a tone of relief, yet low.*

Thank God!

He is gone! he was able to get home. Why, why
Gave I consent to this! If it should kill him!
My God! my God! have pity on his youth!
Giul. Why fear the worst, Madonna? Was he able
To move alone, he is not nigh to death.
Gism. Thou knowest him not, Giulietta. 'T was in longing
To reach, wo 's me! my outstretch'd arms, he fell.
I saw him — dost thou hear me?

> [*grasping Giulietta's arm, and drawing closer
> to her, while her whole body seems to shrink
> together with horror and grief.*

> — clutch three times

At the accursed ropes, ere — ere, sheer down——
Giul. Oh horror! — Dear my lady, how thou tremblest!
Gism. Tremble, girl! —Ere he fell, I say, sheer down,
To the stone pavement. Would the stones have feeling
For his green youth and manly beauty? [*gasping.*] Thou
Saw'st him, as I did, holding his poor head
Press'd 'twixt his hands. Know'st thou what *that*
was for?

> *Pausing, then solemnly and deeply.*

That his blood might not drip upon the marble
Beneath his lady's window, and defame her.
Had he but five minutes left of life and strength,
He had dragg'd himself away, to die elsewhere.

> *She buries her face in her hands
> and sobs — though low.*

After a brief moment, during which GIULIETTA *is seen,
by the dim light of the scene, to gaze on her*

with looks of deep sympathy.
Let not his noble effort for my honor
Be thwarted.   Draw the ladder up.

Giul. Yet hope. [*begins*
to draw the ladder into the chamber.

Gism. Hope? Ay, but pray.   Until thou bring'st, to-
morrow,
Assurance of his safety, shall no pillow
Receive my head, while his — while Aloise's ——

Covers her face again, weeping silently ; and
Scene closes.

<hr/>

Scene III.

A Street.   The houses of Anselmo *and*
Girolamo, *adjoining each other.*
The portal in the basement of one of them is partially open.

Enter,

dragging himself painfully along,

Aloise.

Alo. I can no further.   Here as well to die

As farther off — thy honor sav'd — Gismonda.
        [*Swoons between the two doors.*

Enter

A Captain *of the Signors of the Night*
with twelve Sbirri, and their Lieutenant : *three*
of the men bearing torches.

Capt. What have we here? —   Ho, lights!
        [*They hold the torches over Aloise.*
                Lieut. The Procurator
Marco Foscari's son!
                Capt. The Doge's nephew!
                        Lieut. Bleeding
And — dead, I think.
                Capt. Who can have done this deed?
Go, three of you, and bear him to the Church.
                [*pointing off the scene.*

Two of the Sbirri take up Aloise, *and,*
        another leading with a torch,

                Exeunt.

Whose houses are these, Lieutenant?
                Lieut. The Messeri
Bembo and Barbadico's.   Neither door —
See, Captain, there! [*pushing one back, and opening*
        the other.] is fasten'd.
                Capt. That is strange!

And Messer Foscaro bleeding on the ground ! —
Divide yourselves.   Watch two of you this side,
Two upon that. [*indicating the doors.*
                    Two others go around
To the back wall.   And thou, patrol the street. —
Let nothing out or in. —   Arrest thou [*to the patrol.*
                                    any one
Found lurking. —   If ye [*to the front watch.*
                        hear him sound for help,
One from each side go to him. —   Take one torch,
Lieutenant, and search that house.   I, with the other,
Will enter this.   Quick, fellows, to your posts !

    The watch disperse as distributed.

As the CAPTAIN, *followed by one of the torchbearers,
enters one of the doors, and the* LIEUTENANT, *similarly
        attended, the other, the*

            Scene closes.

SCENE IV.

The Garden — As in Act I., Sc. I., &c.

The Stage is nearly dark.

Enter

on the upper side of the hedge, ISOTTA, —
on the lower, LUTIA ;
both hurriedly.

Isot. [*suppressed tone, but eagerly.*
  Lutia, is 't thou?
     Lut. Isotta, yes.
        Isot. Make haste.
Give me thy hand. Here. Over.
     [*They cross the hedge, changing places.*
        Lut. What 's the matter?
What noise was that in the house?
        Isot. The Devil perhaps.
Did it also come to thine — to mine, that is?
Lut. Tramp, tramp, on the stair. The door was sud-
  denly open'd.
An arm, I think Cassandra's, drew me out.
I saw the light of torches, as I fled,
Flash through the court. I think we are beset.
Isot. And so do I. Our husbands will be caught.

What will they say, when found each in the chamber
Of his sworn foe?

    Lut. And knowing it, as they will!
'T will drive them mad.

      Isot. I cannot help but laugh.

Lut. I had rather cry. But now is time for neither.
 See! Lights iu both houses! *[looking to the right.*

   Isot. [turning to left.] And footsteps in the rear!
Good night, good night. The Devil, if devil it be,
May catch thy husband, but he sha'n't catch me.

         [Exeunt hurriedly
    at their respective sides of the hedge.

    The Drop falls.

Aot the Fourth

Soene I.   *A Cell in the Prisons.*

A sound of bolts and chains withdrawn.
The vaulted door is flung open, and, the Jailer standing by it,

Enter

ANSELMO *and* GIROLAMO
led by the CAPTAIN *and the* LIEUTENANT *of the Watch,*
and followed by six of the Sbirri,
two of them with torches.

Ansel. [*haughtily.*

    Now we are where thou 'dst have us, it may be
Thou 'lt answer us at last, why are we here.
Girol. Come, Captain, this is surely some mistake.
    That gentleman, I will vouch, is, as he told thee,
Messer Anselmo Barbadico ; he
Will say for me, that I am nothing less
Nor worse than I have claim'd to be.   Come, come ;
We are no night-thieves.
              Capt. I might, Messeri both,
Reply, by simply asking you in turn,
Why you, who, all the world of Venice knows,
Are enemies, are found each one by night
In the chamber of the other, and confus'd —

I will not say, in terror, — nor could give
Any account of yourselves why you were there?
This might suffice for Messer Barbadico,
Who I see winces at it.

     Ansel. Hold thy peace:
And know thy place.

  Capt. [*still gravely.*] I know it well enough,
And what the law allows your rank.

       Ansel. Then, peace!
Why we were found where thou hast said, concerns
Ourselves alone. Ourselves alone will answer it,
Each to the other. [*looking significantly at Girol.*
      What is that to thee?

Capt. [*turning to Girol. without further notice of Anselmo.*
  But since you have better feeling, Messer Bembo,
And know the difference 'twixt a dog and me, [*said
      with the same imperturbable gravity.*
I will answer *you*, why I have brought you here.
The Doge's nephew, Aloise Foscaro,
This night was found bath'd in his blood and dead,
On the foundation just before your doors.

  Both start — ANSELMO *less perceptibly.*

You both betray surprise. It may be real,
It may be feign'd. That will appear elsewhere.
Seeing both your doors were open, I had right
To think, perchance involv'd in some amour,
Young Foscaro met his deathwound at the hands
Of some one in your houses. What we found

On entering, I will not offend again,
Messer Girolamo, by repeating here.
Girol. But sir, I do protest ——

                  Capt. I must be pardon'd,
If I refuse your Excellence to hold
Further discourse. My duty here is done.
Ansel. And thou shalt answer for it.

                  Capt. And I will.
I go now to the Signor of the Night
To make report. Until the *Quarantia*
Otherwise order, I shall leave you both
Together and without a special guard. —

                  [*bowing gravely.*
To the right about; in file; and forward, march!

      The Sbirri defile from the cell,
one of the torches leading; and during this movement

            Scene shifts to

SCENE II.

The Interior of a Church.

ALOISE *lying on a bier before the Chancel.*
A small torch at the head, and another at the foot of the bier,
give the only light to the scene.
The CHAPLAIN
is seen in the act of closing one of the church-doors.
He comes forward.

Chapl. Now they are gone, I'll get me to my bed —
'T will yet be warm — and mend my broken sleep.
Giesu! 't is not a trifle to be rous'd
Out of one's dreams at midnight, dreaming too,
Mary forgive us! one of Jerom's dreams,
To enter a cold church. Ugh! Why not let
The dead inter their dead? as Christ's self said.
Midnight? Those torches haply will not burn
Till morning. Should the relatives come in,
And find them out! ——
           Takes two larger torches which are standing
by one of the pillars, and substitutes them. As he is lighting
the one at the head by the one
he has thence removed:
                    Now, Messer Aloise,
I know not if thou wilt see better now ——
9*

Giesu Maria!   St. Fantin! [*dropping the small link
in terror.*] Did he move? [*looking on
the face.*

Oh horror! and all saints! his eyelids open!
*Runs off toward the door, then stops, and, coming
slowly back.*
This is child's terror: if he be alive,
Better for him perhaps, and well for me.
If he be dead, I have seen dead men before,
And bloody ones. [*Lays his hand on Aloise's chest.*
God's holy Cross! he lives!
[*Exit hastily.*
While he is gone, ALOISE *gives certain feeble signs of coming to.*

After a few moments,   .

Enter

the CHAPLAIN,
with another PRIEST *and a* LAY-BROTHER.

Alo. [*without raising his head, and feebly.*
Gismonda! —— [*Again lapses into insensibility.*
Chapl. There! I thought I heard him speak.
Priest. 'T was but thy fancy, brother; and I wish
Thou hadst kept it to thyself: my bed was ready.
Chapl. But here is what will quite[21] thee, were it warm.
As mine was.   Beats his heart, or not?
Priest. It beats!
Let us be quick.   Giuseppe, [*to Lay-brother.*
raise the feet. —

He has swoon'd from loss of blood.

Chapl. Or pain.   So.

[*carrying him off.*

Bear him

Unto my cell.   I am glad my bed is warm.

[*Exeunt with Aloise.*

SCENE III.

The Prison — As in Scene I. of the Act.

The scene is lighted by a lantern on an oaken table.

ANSELMO.   GIROLAMO.

GIROLAMO *is seated on a bench near the table, kicking his heels together, and looking up now and then with an air of drollery at* ANSELMO, *who, with folded arms and head depressed, paces gloomily, at moments fiercely, the cell.*

Ansel. [*suddenly stopping, and, after looking fixedly for a moment or two on Girolamo.*

Messer Girolamo Bembo ——

Girol. [*carelessly.*] Well?

               Ansel. Our sires
Were as our grandsires, and their sires far back,
Great enemies.   I am thinking that they were ——
                                [*pauses.*

Girol. Great fools, perhaps.

           Ansel. Even so.   And since you think ——
'What were you doing, Messerè, in my chamber?

Girol. What were you doing in mine?   It is all one.

Ansel. My lady is a —— Hum! [*clenching his hand fierce-*
                    ly, and resuming his walk.

           Girol. And so is mine. [*kicking*
his heels together—but not carelessly ; then spring-
      ing passionately up and coming forward.

Ansel. You seem to take it easily.

               Girol. Take the devil !
How can I help it?   Any more than this,
That we are thrust together in one cell,
Who hate each other?   Shall we fight it out?
We have no arms.   But there are solid walls,
And here our hands : Your head or mine.   What say
    you?

Ansel. Either you trifle, or you yet not know
Why I now speak who never once before
Open'd my lips to you, and never thought
I ever should.   How look you on our fate?

Girol. As a most damn'd one, take it at the best.

Ansel. And take it at the worst, as we must do,
    'T is this.   To-morrow all of Venice knows

We both are —— Need I breathe the accursed name?

Girol. No, 't is not very amiable.[22]   What then?
How can I help it?

　　　　　Ansel. But what makes it worse,
All Venice knows we are enemies; and, so knowing,
What will it think of what must seem in each
Covert design to wound the other's honor?'
We shall become the laughingstock —

　　　Girol. [*beginning to show uneasiness.*] And scorn —

Ansel. The detestation, and the mere contempt
Of every Pantaloon.[23]

　　　　　Girol. [*somewhat passionately.*

　　　　　Ay.   But again
I say, How can I help it?

He begins to stride across the stage in the manner ANSELMO
had first done.

ANSELMO *watches him a moment in*
the dim light, standing with folded arms.   Then,
slowly, and with depth of tone.

　　　　　Ansel. Help it?   Thus.
We are taken up suspected of the murder
Of Aloise Foscaro.   Let us own it.

Girol. [*stopping short.*
　　　Art thou in earnest?

　　　　　Ansel. Earnest?   Am I one
Was ever known to utter words in jest?

Girol. No, by St. Jerom!   Monna Lutia took
Your sober earnest seriously to heart.

Ansel. That is an ill-tim'd pleasantry, Messerè.

Girol. It cost me dear then.   It was devilish bitter,
   Like John's book, in my belly.[24]   Thou may'st cap it
   With one on me and Isotta, if thou like.
Ansel. [*with clenched hand, and stamping the floor.*
      Damn her !
         Girol. Ay, damn them both, loose jades !
                        Ansel. Amen !
   From the bottom of my soul !   But were they damn'd
   Effectually by our wish, that saves us not
   From the deep hell of infamy wherein
   Their known incontinence plunges, for all time,
   The body of our honor: for all time !
   A moral stench and fire to which the gulf
   Of Dante's horridest Circle were mild Eden.
   Think'st thou not so ?
            Girol. [*with much feeling.*]
                Peace I name it not, Anselmo.
Ansel. [*at first shrinking.*
      Anselmo ? — [*brief hesitation.*
            But 't is well.   For thou art hearty ;
   And I believe our grandsires were great fools.
   Girolamo Bembo, — 't is thy enemy speaks,
   Thy enemy that was, but who will be
   Truly thy friend a few brief hours of life,
   If so thou wilt, — thou wouldst not live to bear
   The slur of obloquy, the pitying shrug,
   The mocking smile, the whisper and the joke :
   "That 's he !   Lucretia-Lutia's merry keeper."
   "Messer Girolamo; how 's thy enemy's rib ?"

Girol. [who has been patting the floor with his foot, his lips
sternly compressed.
Anselmo Barbadico ——
                    Ansel. [purposely disregarding him.
                    —— Wouldst not bear
To know thou own'dst a wife who ——
                    more quickly.] Wouldst thou bear
To be so damn'd, and daily ?
                    Girol. Would I live
To lose the all for which life 's worth the living ;
Decent opinion and a happy heart ?
Better a thousand deaths !
                    Ansel. It is but one.
I 'll share it with thee.   Touch my hand.
                    Girol. [at first shrinking as Ansel. had done —
                    then, with great frankness and putting
                    . his whole hand into Anselmo's.
                    I will.
This morning I had clasp'd the Devil's as soon.
Ansel. We meant to wrong each other, and, so meaning,
Did wrong each other.   Let us now each other
Right, and that nobly.   One thing is resolv'd :
Young Foscari died by our joint hands, detected
In infamous commerce with our strumpet wives.
The how and when, and wherefore we were found —
Where we were found, — that must we now revolve ;
That not the horrors of the Question force
One word from our parch'd throats, to give the lie
To each other's story.

Girol. Let them wrench our limbs:
Our heart's pang has a bloodier sweat. — But hark:
Is 't right to blacken Foscaro, that ourselves
May be made whiter?

   Ansel. Wherefore not? He sleeps:
He will not hear it; and he fell, no doubt,
By some avenger's hand; while our damn'd wives
Get but their due.

   Girol. Ay, damn them! Venice too,
That breeds such vermin!

   Ansel. Rather damn ourselves,
Who fancied each his footing solid ground,
While grinning at his neighbor's floor of glass.[25]

They walk up to the table, and GIROLAMO *appears to arrange
the lantern on it so that they may sit on either
side ; and Scene closes.*

SCENE IV.

The Sleeping-Chamber of the Chaplain.

ALOISE *lying back in an easy chair; two* SURGEONS *on either side him, one holding his wrist. His head is bandaged. He is deadly pale, and his eyes are closed.*

M. DOMENICO MARIPETRO, *Signor of the Night.* —
The CHAPLAIN.—*His fellow* PRIEST. — *The* LAY-BROTHER.

All but the LAY-BROTHER
come forward, leaving ALOISE *a little in the background.*

1st Sur. You now may question him, Messer Maripetro.
2d Sur. [*who had held Aloise's wrist.*
        So it be gently, and at no great length.
Marip. I understand you truly then, Messeri,
    These wounds are come of accident, — from a fall,
    Not from premeditated violence?
                    1st Sur. No.
    Even without the bruises and abrasions   ·
    Which mark the patient's body and his palms,
    We should not deem him wounded by assault. —
2d Sur. Although it is not impossible.
                    1st Sur. Although —
    As thinks my learned brother — presupposing
    Certain conditions of weapon and attack,
    It yet might be. But doubt is put at rest,

By the distinguish'd patient's own avowal.

[turning to the Chapl.

Chapl. 'T is so.   His Excellence has avow'd he fell

From a balcony of the Casa Mora.

Marip. Seem'd he to have his senses when he spoke?

Chapl. It might be; and again, it might be not.

'T was waking from his swoon.   The avowal made,

He gave a cry of pain and swoon'd again.

1st Sur. With pardon of his Reverence be it said,

The cry was more of terror or despair,

As though in the flutter of returning sense

He had utter'd what was perilous to reveal.²⁶

Chapl. 'Tis very likely: I am growing old.

Messer Aloise! — *[going up to Alo.*

Marip. Hush! — *[goes up also.   The rest*

follow.

Messerè, *[to Alo. — Aloise*

opens his eyes, and again closes them.

You fell, you have said, from Messer Moro's window.

Alo. *[leaning forward.*

I did. — O fatal slip! *[to himself. —   He strikes*

his hands together, and falls back, and groans.

1st Sur. *[to Marip.]* There!   Said I right?²⁷

Marip. *[waving his hand to impose silence.*

Know you me, Messer Aloise Foscari?

I am one of the Signori of the Night,

Doménico Maripetro.   Two young nobles

Were seiz'd on mere suspicion of your murder,

And are detain'd to answer for the attempt.

Will you absolve them? Whence had you these wounds?
ALOISE *turns uneasily in the chair.*
A pause.
What took you to the Casa Mora windows,
Since it must be you were in secret there?
Another pause.
Alo. [*heavily sighing.*
    Let not the innocent suffer. I must die,
And will not keep this secret on my breast
Which is half utter'd. Ser Giovanni Moro,
Whose wealth is known, keeps constantly in his house
Large sums of money, and has hoarded jewels
Of vast amount, whose storing-place I knew.
A pause. The attendants, &c.,
gaze on him with intense interest. He keeps his eyes
still closed.
Observing that the windows in the rear,
Which light the corridors, were night and day
In the warm season open, I resolv'd
This night to scale them.
Again a pause — the company
gazing on him with an expression of increasing interest, which
now partakes of alarm and even horror.
                      At the fourth hour then,
With a mask'd lantern arm'd and certain keys
Whose master wards would open every lock,
I threw a rope-ladder to the mid balcony
Of the mid floor, where stood a casement open,
And mounted. [*He pauses.*

Chapl. O ye saints, and San Fantino!
O horror, and Jesus-Mary! And a noble!

The other PRIEST *and the* LAY-BROTHER
*cross themselves. The Surgeons exchange looks
of dismay,* 1st *Surgeon's mingled with an expression
of doubt.* MARIPETRO *keeps his eyes on* ALOISE, *giving no
other sign of emotion than the knitting of his brows.
He waves, however, his hand again, to impose
silence on the* CHAPLAIN.

Alo. The claws were not well grappled to the rails :
My weight drew down the ladder; and I fell.
Wounded and bleeding, half-wild with fear and shame,
I had the strength to sink in the Canal
My implements, and staggering sought my home.
But overcome with pain and loss of blood,
I soon lay down to die. I know no more.
Chapl. The Doge's nephew robbing! Holy Cross!

MARIPETRO, *gazing a moment fixedly on*
ALOISE (*who keeps always his eyes shut*), *turns round and
looks upon the bystanders.* 1ST SURGEON *betrays
strong incredulity.*

Marip. 'T is a strange story, Messer Aloise ;
And be it not disprov'd 't will cost you dear.
Robbery has of late been fearful-rife,
And the strong hand of law must put it down.
Your uncle will not shield you.
                              Alo. Let him not.

I can but die, and shall perhaps even here.

Chapl. The Lord vouchsafe your Excellence better thoughts!

As this is said, 1ST SURGEON *draws*
MARIPETRO *forward.*

1st Sur. I think his senses wander.

Marip. Yet the tale
Was congruous and coherent. And his wounds?

1st Sur. I have never doubted came from some such fall.
I doubt his motives.

Marip. These the law will search.

[*Returning to Alo.*

My painful duty, Messer Aloise,
Must be discharg'd. —

Alo. Discharge it. I complain not.

Marip. Your father sent for will be shortly here.
Meantime I leave you with a single guard,
Who shall await without. [*going.*

Alo. Receive my thanks.

Enter, MARCO FOSCARI.

Marip. The Procurator is already come.

Alo. Father! [*painfully.*

Fosc. My son ! How is it with thee now?

Alo. Poorly in mind and body. I have made [*faintly.*
Confession of my guilt.

Fosc. Thy guilt ! He raves !
Speak, Maripetro !

Marip. 'T is indeed too true.
Your Excellency's son admits to have fallen

In an attempt — I am sorry so to speak —
To rob the Casa Mora.

> *Fosc.* He is mad! [*gazing anxiously*
> *on Alo. who keeps his eyes closed.*

1*st Sur.* For the moment — partially. He should have rest.
Bewilderment of the cerebral functions
Has follow'd the concussion, as did syncope
The blood's congestion.

> *Fosc.* [*motioning to the company to go.*
> Give me leave, good friends.

Thou dost not fear to leave me, Maripetro,
Alone with Aloise?

> MARIPETRO *bows,*
> *and Exit with the others by a door.*
> Aloise!

Art in thy senses?

> *Alo.* Never more so, father.

Fosc. What hast thou done then? Whence and how this
    fall?
What took thee to Giovanni Moro's house?

Alo. Attempting to ascend a high balcony;
With what intention, spare me to repeat.

Fosc. Degenerate boy! Art thou so lost to shame?
Open thine eyes, and look me in the face.
Thou cast'st them down! Is 't guilt? This is some
    cheat!
The tenor of thy past life shows it so.
Thou hast been noble, generous, from a child,
Oblivious of thyself for others' good,

Incapable of avarice: thou art Foscaro.
The tears are gushing from thy clos'd eyes fast!
My own begin to trickle. O my son !
What is thy trouble? Fear not! Come; confess.
Thou didst not fall; thou wast hurl'd down perhaps
From some high window, caught in some amour.
Make me thy friend: I will not judge thee harshly.
Alo. [*much moved*
>   My father !——
>   *Fosc.* [*caressingly.*
>   Yes, yes; that is it.
>   *Alo.* [*despairingly.*
>   No, no!
It is in vain. Let justice have its course.
Ask me no more.
>   *Fosc.* Let justice have its course?
Art thou a villain then? And wilt thou hang?
Alo. No, I shall die before the cord be ready.
Fosc. But, dying so, thou wilt not save our shame.
Thou art the Doge's nephew, and my son.
Thou art no villain. Either thou art mad,
With thy wounds' fever, or there lies here hid
Some mystery, perhaps of love-intrigue,
Which I shall know to fathom. Rest in peace.
I go to the Ducal Palace straight.
>   [*Exit by the door.*
>   *Alo.* Gismonda!
I have stripp'd my honor bare, to cover thine.
>   [*Swoons*

Enter, from the door,
MARIPETRO, CHAPLAIN, *and* SURGEONS.
The PRIEST *and* LAY-BROTHER
behind.

Chapl. [*as he crosses the sill.*
O borror! and St. Job! he is gone again!

1st Sur. It has been too much for him.

                 2d Sur. As I foresaw.

The SURGEONS *and* CHAPLAIN *hastily,* MARIPETRO
slowly, move towards ALOISE. *The*
PRIEST *and* LAY-BROTHER *press*
through the door.
And during this movement the

Drop falls.

ACT THE FIFTH

SCENE I. *In the Ducal Palace. The Hall of the
Council of Ten.*

LOREDANO, MOCENIGO
*and others of the Council assembled.
The* DOGE *presiding.*

Doge. Illustrious Signors! Now the affairs of state
Which call'd you hither are over, ere we part
Give me your sufferance. If we call your bearing
From the deep thunder of the Milan war
To meaner trouble and scarce audible sound
Whose near reverberations startle rarely
The far-removed sphere of your high functions,
It is not idly. In the affair we indicate
There is a mystery, and a double plot
Darkly inwoven, and so close-perplex'd,
As needs to unravel it your graver judgment
And your supreme authority to resolve, —
The honor of three noble houses being
Therein involv'd. Vouchsafe us then your patience.
Have we your high permission to proceed.
    The COUNCIL *exchange looks of inquiry, then
        gravely nod assent.*
'T is known in Venice, Aloise Foscaro,
VOL. IV.—10

Many weeks since, was taken up for dead
Between the open portals of two houses;
Girolamo Bembo's being one, the other
Anselmo Barbadico's.   Search being made,
These nobles — foes, observe! were found in the dark
Each in the other's house, at dead of night.
Charg'd with the seeming murder, each apart
Avow'd for himself, seeing Aloise pass
At certain hours often by their doors,
And knowing their wives were faithless, they had lain
That night in wait for him, unknown to each other,
And, rushing out together, between them slain him.
Hearing then the tramp and seeing from afar
The torches of the night-guard, scar'd, bewilder'd,
Having chang'd their places in the assault, they fled
Each through the other's portal unawares, —
Their houses being similar.   That the wounded
Died not, makes not their story false.   But lo!
Being question'd, Aloise avers he fell
From a balcony of the Casa Mora,
Attempting — who will credit such a tale?
To rob the house!

          Loredano. Why not?   What 's in a Foscaro,
Should save him from the crimes of vulgar men?
Doge. Nothing: but much to keep him from their mean-
     ness.
Lored. What 's that? the Ducal Bonnet?
                       Doge. No; but that
Which we might say a Loredano wants

Since the brave Admiral, Pietro of that name,
Stoops to offend the feelings of an uncle
To gratify the malice of his hate.
Mocenigo. [*hastily.*
    What said they to this strange avowal ?
Doge. [*bowing to Mocen. and then around the ·Council.*
                         Pardon :
The trodden worm will turn ; I cannot kiss
My enemy's heel. —   They affirm'd it was delusion ;
Delirium from the fever of his wounds. —
By order of the Criminal Quarantía,
Search being made in the Canal from Moro's
To Barbadico's house, was nothing found,
Though Aloise said therein he threw
A ladder, keys, and lantern. He avers
Still to have fallen ; still the two maintain
Their story of assault.
             Mocen. With what design ?
Doge.   To find in death a refuge from dishonor.
Disgusted with their wives, and sick of life,
Made friends by common suffering, they plann'd,
In their deep passion and shame, what now for shame
They scruple to retract.
           Mocen. And Aloise ?
Doge.   Doubtless did fall ; but from what house and how,
Lies yet in darkness.   .
        Lored. Give them to the rack. ·
All three will render up their secrets straight.
Their folly or guilt needs not this high tribunal

To sift or punish it.

    Doge. 'T is because the rack
Threatens now needlessly their youthful limbs,
We crave in their behalf the Council's favor —
To us, not them.   Our Procurator brother
Has found a clue to Aloise's part,
In certain feeble hints Giovánni Moro,
Close-question'd, gave him.   Grant us ample power
To search this matter, we pledge our faith to make it
Clear as noon-day, the issue leaving wholly
To your high verdict. [*he speaks still to the rest of the
        Council, without regarding Loredano.*

    Lored. As is simply fit.
The Doge would seek immunity for his nephew
And brother's son.

    Doge. The Doge before the Ten
Knows not his brother nor his brother's son.
Francesco Foscari is servant of the State.
When was he ever known to scant his duty ?
When to refuse a sacrifice of self ?
Not only his nephew, does the law demand him,
But his own children ; he surrenders all ;
Even dead will ye have it so.

    Lored. [*muttered.*] It yet may be.[28]

Mocen. I see no power that may not well be granted
Unto his Highness in this strange affair.
Why should the noble Admiral refuse
To do his enemy justice ?

    Lored. I refuse not.

Is it the pleasure of the rest, 't is mine.

Mocen. Is it agreed then ? [*looking round upon the Council.*

All the members nod affirmatively except

Lored., who remains motionless.

It is granted. [*to the Doge.*

Doge. [*bowing acknowledgment.*] Thanks. —

Associates, the Council stands adjourn'd.

COUNCIL, *rising, prepare to separate as*

Scene closes.

SCENE II.

A room in the house of Anselmo.

ISOTTA.   LUTIA.

Lut. Is there to be no end to this suspense ?

Isot. Why soon, I think.   Now Aloise Foscari

Is well enough to stand before a court,

The trial must come on.

Lut. And then ?

Isot. Why then,
What but our lords' release?   Has Foscaro been
Too noble to avow the rightful source
Of his disaster — which I think was hardly
Our friend Gismonda's jewels, — will he seek
For safety in our husbands' wild invention?
Its falsehood obvious, they are free.

Lut. To vent
The vengeance of their prisonment on us.

Isot.   We soon will turn the tables on them.   What!
Did they not bring it on themselves?   'T is little
Indeed atonement for their sins!   And we?
Have we gone scathless?   Not the humblest soul
Of all our husbands' lineage, scarce a friend
Or relative of our own, to touch our hands
Or hold communion with us!   Both set down,
In a vile city, as the vilest vile!

Enter,

CASSANDRA, *precipitately,*

with looks of dismay.

What now?   What is it, girl?

Cass. O God! Madonna!

Isot.   Why dost thou wring thy hands?   What hast thou
    heard?
What seen?

Cass. Seen nothing — not as yet.   But see
The town will soon. —   O dear! O dear! my master!

Isot.   What of him ?   Speak !

                    Lut.   And of my lord ?

                           Cass.   They are both

Condemn'd to lose their heads between the pillars. —

Isot. [*jocosely, and sustaining Lutia, who appears dumb
   with horror.*

    Don't faint, my Lutia!

                   Cass. [*looking on Isotta with surprise.*

                Really though, Madonna! ——

Isot.   I do not doubt it.   They 're to lose their heads ;
And ? ——

        Cass. Messer Aloise to be hung.

Isot.   Ha, ha, ha !

        Cass. But it is true.

                  Lut. Isotta! ——

Isot..   Now, don't give way !   Here comes Giovanna too,

                     Enter,

           with like discomposure,

                GIOVANNA.

We will hear her first.   Well !   didst thou see them die ?

Giov. [*in extremity of surprise.*

    Madama !

             Lut. Mind her not, Giovanna !   Speak !

What is this horrid story ?

                   Giov. 'T is too true.

I had it from the porter.   And I came

Straightway to tell you.   And I found the men

In the court below were talking of it too.

Isot. [*making a gesture to restrain Lutia, who looks wildly
    from Giov. to Isot.*

Talking of what?—   Now, Lutia, do be still!

Giov. 'T is talk'd all over Venice—so they say.
Madonna Lutia's, and your lord, Madonna,
Will be beheaded in the Piazzetta,
And the Duke's nephew hung.

                              Isot. Right wisely done!

Hail Francis Foscaro, the new Solomon!

Lut. God keep us sane!   This horror drives her wild!

Isot. No, joy.—Thou hast heard how Solomon the Jew,
To find the mother, where two claim'd a child,
Order'd the little bantling cut in two.
So Solomon the Venetian, to discover
The entangled secret of our *Double Deceit*,
Proposes to behead each *Husband-Lover*,
And hang his nephew in the public street.
Nay, never stare!   'T is so, and wisely done.
Hail Francis Foscaro, the new Solomon!

Lut. Do leave thy rhymes, Isotta; and disclose
Thy meaning plainly.

                              Isot. Plainly, in plain prose:
Come with me to Gismonda.

                              Lut. With what view?

Hop'st thou she would admit us *now?*   .

                              Isot. I do.
Cassandra shall prepare the way.

                              Lut. Her sire

___

Will shut the door in our faces.

                Isot. He sha'n't see them.

We will go mask'd. Now, not a word, my dear!

'T is time for action now, not speech. Go bid

The gondola be prepar'd, Cassandra.

                      Lut. No.

'T is but a step. We had better walk.

                   Isot. The barge

Will screen us better while we wait without.

                        [*Exit Cass.*

Come to my closet. I have masks for both.

      They move towards a door.

I hardly think, my dear, the Doge will care

To chop two heads off 'twixt the two stone pillars,.

Because they wish'd to choose 'twixt two down

    pillows.

Lut. No; Venice would have nought but bodies then.

Isot. Save a few heads — of children and old men.

Lut. O monstrous libel! Would no women keep

    Their heads then on their shoulders?

                  Isot. Some — asleep.

Lut. What then do we awake in this Lot's town?

Isot. O, we are friends, and spare each other's down.

             [*Opens the door, and in the act*

                   Scene changes.

10*

SCENE III.

In the house of Giovanni Moro,

As in Act II., Sc. III.

MORO. GISMONDA.

Moro. I will have nought to do with it, I say.
Thou hast disobey'd me; and, by thy connivance,
Young Foscari would have forc'd his way by night
Into my house— I do believe, Gismonda,
.   From thy own nobleness, not to thy dishonor—
              GISMONDA *raises his hand*
        to her lips. MORO *draws it away with*
              affected roughness.
Now, none of that! unless it be in token
Of penitence for the past. I say, Gismonda.
If Aloise did not enter here,
It was by his misfortune, not thy fault;
And though thou 'scap'st the forfeit, he shall not;
Not by my movement.
              Gism. And his self-denial?
Father, thou call'dst it noble. Canst thou wish
To punish him through the very merit which won
But now thy favor?
              Moro. I punish not. I own,
The youth is brave, is noble, is magnanimous,

Is worthy of his name: but is 't my fault
He lost his balance? I would have pitch'd him down,
Had I been near him. Let him pay the cost
Of his mad passions, as all men must do
Sometime or other.

    Gism. It is done, my father.
Frightful atonement! He has barely 'scap'd
Alas! with life.

    Moro. So let his broken bones
Teach him a lesson. I will not intercede
With his stern uncle. I have done enough,
Avowing to his father that he knew thee.
Hang him or not, I wash my hands of all.

Gism. Yet, for my sake, for mine! dear father, pity!

Moro. Thou art a fool — or feign'st to be. Thou knowest,
As well as I do, Foscari will not hang.
He has risk'd his neck to save thy honor; and thou,
I doubt it not, wilt risk thy honor in turn
To save his neck. But if thou do, remember,
I have no part in it! And —— What is this?

    Enter GIULIETTA.

Giul. May it please Madonna, a girl without craves leave
Of speech with her.

    Moro. Admit her: I have done.

        [*Exit Giul.*

Now bear in mind, Gismonda! I 'll not stir
A hand to save him, let him hang or not.

      [*Exit Moro — in opposite direction.*

Re-enter GIULIETTA *with* CASSANDRA.

GISMONDA, *on seeing the latter, turns indignantly on*
GIULIETTA.

Cass. Madonna, pardon me: you have no cause
　To look displeas'd.　I have indeed been sent——
Gism. [*gravely.*
　What does thy mistress want with me, Cassandra?
Cass. It is a matter that concerns you both.
　　　　　　GISMONDA *draws herself up,*
　　　　but with more displeasure than disdain.
　Nay, you do wrong her, Madam.　On my word,
　She is innocent, and as virtuous as yourself.
Gism. Girl!——　Come. [*to Giul., and moving off.*
　　● *Cass.* Do hear me!　Do be just!
　　　　　　　　　　　Giul. Do hear!
　Appearances, Madonna, may deceive.
Cass. [*significantly.*
　Madonna Mora's self might be misjudg'd.
Gism. Ah! say'st thou?　Well; be brief.
　　　　　　　　　Cass. Then briefly, thus:
　My master and Madonna Bembo's lord
　Made love to each other's spouse.　The ladies told
　Immediately each the other, and contriv'd
　To assume each other's place.
　　　　　　　　Gism. Ah! truly?
　　　　　　　　　　Cass. Madam,
　I and Madonna Lutia's maid, Giovanna,
　Were cognizant of all and help'd in all.

Gism. Could I believe thee !
               Cass. That needs not.   My lady
Brings her own proof.
               Gism. What mean'st thou ?
                   Cass. They are come,
She and Madonna Lutia, to concert
Measures with you to rescue all the three,
Their husbands and the nephew of the Doge.
Will you not see them ?
               Giul. [*Gismonda hesitating.*
           See them, dear my lady :
The Devil is not so black as he is drawn.
Cass.   They are no devils at all.
               Giul. That 's true ; being come
Upon an errand of mercy.
               Gism. Thou distract'st me :
Peace ! — [*A pause.   Considering.*
   To Cass.] I will see them. —
             Go thou with Cassandra.
             [*Exit Giul. and Cass.*
    GISMONDA *walks thoughtfully to and fro*
          a few moments.
'T is very true.   Myself might be misjudg'd.
I have but Giulietta to maintain
My plea of honor.   Why should I distrust
Isotta, still more Lutia?   If the world
Traduce them for their husbands' fault, may 't not,
When I relate for Aloise's sake
My story of the rendezvous, believe

Me too impure?   The trial will come hard.
But thou didst venture all, thou gallant spirit!
Why should not I?   Albeit the risk for me
Is more than death.

Enter

ISOTTA *and* LUTIA,
wearing masks, which they immediately remove,
CASSANDRA, GIULIETTA, *and* GIOVANNA.
*These three retire to the background, and, during the colloquy
between their mistresses,* GIULIETTA, *in dumb-show,
appears by her gesticulations (pointing to
the window, &c.) to be recounting
the misfortune of* ALOISE.

> *Isot.* Salute us not, Gismonda.
Spare us a welcome that must needs be cold.
Lut.   And yet it should not.   Why shouldst thou accept,
Who knowest us, all a lying world puts forth?
Gism. Your husbands did. [*Gism. speaks, though gravely
and with sufficient firmness, yet with diffidence.*
> *Isot.* Our husbands were deceiv'd.
Has not Cassandra told thee?
> *Gism.* [*same manner.*] But in brief.
'T was a strange tale. She said thou hadst the proofs.
Isot.   Which we shall lay before the Duke himself.
Thou she - St. Thomas! thou shalt put thy fingers
Upon the very marks.
> *Lut.* O dear Gismonda!
What better proof than that our coming brings?

Were we so guilty, wouldst thou see us here?
Look in our faces.

       Isot. It is aptly urg'd.
But I may claim to add: What, did we say
Young Foscaro——

       Gism. No, no! do not say it! no!
Forgive me! We will not distrust each other; not
On the world's showing only. [*Gives a hand to each.*

       Isot. Now then, hear
Why we are come. What think'st thou means the
   Doge?
It were preposterous, tyranny unmatch'd,
To put to death, even on their own confession,
Two men of standing, for a night-assault,
When the pretended victim swears himself
'T was never made. The Doge then would discover,
Why this self-accusation; why two foes
Were found at midnight each in the other's chamber;
Why his own nephew, hitherto unstain'd,
Takes on himself a crime not less degrading
Than heinous. In a word, the Doge, my dear,
Would bring us out, sagaciously divining
We three could solve this mystery if we would.
The Doge must have his will.

       Gism. But how, Isotta?
Isot. We must appeal to him — appear before him,
If he desire. There is no other way,
Especially for thee. But tell us frankly:⁻
Thou art the jewel young Foscari came to rob?

Fie! never blush; the world must know it soon.

Gism. My father had forbidden him the house.

Isot. Ah? — But the why concerns not us. — Thy sire
Knows then of all, and knowing can explain.

Gism. But that he will not do: he swears it roundly.
His stubborn humor — if I must call it so —
Thou knowest.

   Lut. But hast thou not some friend, Gismonda,
Will speak for thee, and us? our cause being one.
For this we are come. For we are stripp'd of friends
By our misfortune.

    Isot: Nor will stoop to plead
Through any advocate for that mere justice
That should be meted us on our own asking,
And the bare statement of the naked facts.

Gism. So it becomes you best. — [*Considering.*] I know
of one.

There is Stef'ano Moceni'go, of the Ten.

Isot. Who better? 'T is the Doge's single friend
In a malignant and opposing Council.
Let us prepare a letter to the Prince,
Requesting in the names of all the three
An instant hearing. This, dispatch'd forthwith,
The Minister will bear him. Let us haste.
The College sits to-day: there is bare time
To find the Doge alone.

    Lut. And not an hour,
For the three prisoners' sake and for our own,
To throw away: the town is in a ferment.

Gism. Come to my oratory then; for here
  My father might break in and interrupt us.
Isot. And catch without our masks us, wicked pair,
  And wonder how the devil we got here.

> GISMONDA *leads them to the door of a cabinet,*
>   *which opening, she shows them in.*

Cass. Be not concern'd, fair ladies: if 't will do,
  I and Giovanna here will mask for you.

> [*Exit Lutia.*

Isot. [*looking back.*

  Thou 'dst better it, thou jade! — Here wait ye two
Our coming back. And keep your faces bare.

> [*Exit, followed by*
> *Gismonda, who, in character, has looked*
>   *rather surprised; and door closes.*

Giul. — For Master's eyes.

> *To Cass.*] Charm'd with that modest air,
He 'll think it better pastime here to sue,
Than join the ladies yonder at their prayer.

> GIULIETTA *and* CASSANDRA *put on the masks*
> *and begin to caricature the airs of fine ladies to the*
>   *amusement of* GIOVANNA; *and*

> *Scene closes.*

SCENE IV.

THE PIAZZETTA.

The same concourse as in Act I., Sc. II.; but the groups are
earnestly conversing and gesticulating, and a knot
of people stands in apparent expectation
about the portal of the Palace.

In the foreground, an OLD WOMAN *coming down the stage,*
and a GONDOLIER *going up from the left.*

Enter,
from the right, ISOTTA *and* LUTIA,
attended by CASSANDRA *and* GIOVANNA.

Old Wom. [*observing them.*
        Hoot, the bold hussies!
Gondol. [*facing about at the cry.*
                        Give them a wide berth;
They 've got men's blood on them.
                        Old Wom. Or soon will have.
Isot. [*firmly, yet in an under tone.*
        Fear them not, Lutia; we shall soon be through. —
Keep close to us, girls.

Enter
the two SURGEONS.

1st *Sur.* [*to Gondol.*] What is this all about?
Gondol. [*crying out to Isot., &c.*
        Take care of the columns![20] Ye have brought already

Two gallant men betwixt them, ye foul jades!

2d Sur. [to 1st Sur.

'T is the two wives of the condemn'd young nobles,
Bembo and Barbadico.   One I know.

*Gondol. [who has turned about to the Surgeons, after the
above obloquy.*

Then you 've a bad acquaintance.

*Old Wom. [hobbling after Isot.,
&c., and gesticulating.]* Stone the jades!

*Gondol. [who has given attention to this cry, now half-
turning again to the Surgeons.*

I wish I had them bound upon a plank
Well-charg'd with stones, between two gondolas!
Would n't the boats part quickly![30]

Old Wom. [still pursuing.

Stone the jades!

*[And the crowd in the background
take up the cry : "Stone them!"
The ladies are seen to cower.*

Gondol. [running up.

I 'll see the muss.

1st Sur. [seriously to 2d Sur.

They are in great danger.

Enter a body of SBIRRI
with CAPTAIN.

Capt. Halt! —

Back, ye mad fools! Disperse, ye hags! — Left wheel!
Forward!

The Archers march up the stage, and, the mob
sullenly retiring, the ladies, &c., continue on their
way to the Ducal Palace, which presently (in the course of
the Scene) they enter.

1st *Sur.* [*in tone of relief.*

In time!

Gondol. The Devil take the Sbirri!
They 're always in the way, those fellows! — Who 's
this ?

Enter from the left
GISMONDA *and* GIOVANNI MORO
and GIULIETTA.
They pass slowly up the stage towards the Palace (which they
enter before the close of the Scene.)
Directly after them, also from the left,
the CHAPLAIN.

Chapl. [*to Gondol.*

Hush, my brave Barcarole! that 's Messer Moro.
And the young lady, my brave Barcarole,
Is Messer Moro's daughter, Monna Mora.
They are going before the Doge. —

Gondol. O yes, I know,
To inform against his brigand, cut-throat nephew.
She 's a brave lady!   He 's a villain!

1st *Sur.* What for ?

Gondol. What for, my citizen ?   If seven big murders
For a young fellow, like Aloise Foscaro,
Be not enough to make a villain! ——

Chapl. Seven!

O horror! and St. Moses!   Why, my son,

He ne'er committed one!

Gondol. So much thou knowest,

Good Father!   I say, seven.

Old Wom. Nay, 't was eight!

Did n't he stick Madonna Mora's maid?

Gondol. St. Peter! no!   I 'll tell ye about that.

He got up by a ladder with a torch,—

Meaning to fire the house, to rob it safely.

But, by good luck, Madonna Mora's maid,—

That 's she behind her — a right buxom lass! ——

Old Wom. She walks like a crab.

Gondol. Thou 'rt crabb'd thyself, old wench;

A soft crab!

Old Wom. Am I! thou salt-water hog!

I 'll let thee feel my claws!

Gondol. Keep off, old mermaid!

I 'll put my oar to thy flippers, an' thou don't. —

Well, by good luck, Messeri, as I said,

The maid lay with a toothache wide-awake,

And, seeing the light, awoke her sleeping lady.

They stole to the balcony.   Then the maid

Dashing the blazing pine in 's face, the lady

Tripp'd-up the ladder.   Wa'n't it bravely done?

And so we shall see this Princes-nephew hung.

Come on, old crab!   Three cheers for Monna Mora!

Goes up the stage,

OLD WOMAN *hobbling after him threateningly.*

1st Sur. And, Down with the Prince's nephew! if he durst.

Chapl. Giesu! was ever! — But I 'm growing old!
    Seven murders!

       1st Sur. "Nay, 't was eight." For, " didn't he stick
    Madonna Mora's maid?"

           2d Sur. With lighted torch.

Chapl. Ah! popular rumor! popular rumor, sons!

1st Sur. Is a soft-shell crab, of our Gondolier's description.
    It climbs too high sometimes our mansion-walls:
    Then ebbs the tide, and the oozy crawler 's left
    Out of his element. — For the Palace, Father?

Chapl. Ay, gentle son. Perhaps I may be needed
    Before the College, in Foscari's behalf.
    I heard him mutter some things much like love
    And Monna Mora's name in his fever once.
    But I am growing old now.

       1st Sur. So are we.

2d Sur. And bound for the Palace too, with similar views.

Chapl. Come then, my sons. St. Fantin, and all saints!
    'T were a great shame, to hang a Doge's nephew.

1st Sur. Slight fear of that, good Chaplain. 'T is a sham:
    A plummet let down in the well of Truth.

Chapl. Think'st thou? 'T is likely. But I 'm getting old.
    St. Christopher! they must not hang him yet,
    If we can help it. Come away, fair sons.

      They move up the stage, and

        Scene closes.

SCENE V., AND THE LAST.

In the Ducal Palace. The Hall of the College.

On the right, in his robes of state, and crowned with the
Ducal Corno, the DOGE *on his throne between his* SIX
COUNSÉLORS *of the College, — having before him* 'LORE-
DANO, MOCENIGO, *and others of the* COUNCIL OF TEN.
In the background, the CRIMINAL QUARANTI'A, *and others*
of the COLLEGE. *In front of them, standing, the* AVVO-
GADORE MOROSINI. — *In the centre of the stage, somewhat*
back, stands ALOISE, *with two* SBIRRI *behind him leaning*
on their pikes, MARCO FOSCARO *on his right hand, and*
MARIPETRO, *a little behind him, on his left. — More for-*
ward, and somewhat to the left of ALOISE, BEMBO *and*
BARRADICO, *with four* SBIRRI *and the* CAPTAIN OF THE
NIGHT. *Near the left wing, far down in the foreground,*
the CHAPLAIN *and the two* SURGEONS (*who enter however*
during the DOGE's *speech*).

Doge. By your advice, most learn'd and noble Counselors,
The other members of this potent College
Giving consent — our brothers of the Ten
Therein conjoin'd, by whose illustrious sanction
This strange affair (which from its private nature,
Affecting individuals not the State,
Concerns a portion rather of your body,
The Criminal Forty, than the exalted whole)[31]

Was given to us to manage at our will
For the great ends of justice and the good
Of the aggriev'd concern'd, — by your joint order
And liberal sufferance, shall we now proceed
To loose the tangles of this intricate plot,
For whose unravelment all Venice waits
Impatiently.   The prisoners stand before you.
Two parties, who profess to hold the key •
To unlock this mystery, attend without.
Is it your pleasure they be summon'd in
And questioned?

> *The* Doge *looks around the assembly,*
> *which gravely bowing,*
> *he motions with his hand, and*

Enter

Isotta *and* Lutia, *attended by* Cassandra *and* Giovanna;
then, after a brief interval, Gismonda,
leaning on Moro's *arm, and followed by* Giulietta.

As Isotta *passes before* Anselmo, *she throws at him a sidelong look of malicious pleasure, which* Anselmo *returns
with one of concentrated indignation.* Girolamo *glances
with a half-impatient half-careless look at* Lutia, *who
however keeps down her head.   He then exchanges looks
with* Anselmo, *who clenches passionately his hand, —
without however lifting it.*

Ye, who answer for the Ser
Anselmo Barbadico and the Ser

Girolamo Bembo, stand befor our throne.

The other dame be seated.

> GISMONDA, *after mutely endeavoring to per-*
> *suade* MORO *to remain by her (pressing his hand*
> *in both of hers, &c.), takes a seat which is offered,*
> *first exchanging a timid and anxious look with*
> ALOISE, *who appears deeply moved.* GIULIETTA
> *stands up behind her chair.* MORO *has retired*
> *close to the left wing of the scene, before* GIS-
> MONDA *sits, and stands near the* CHAPLAIN *and*
> SURGEONS.

Now, fair ladies,

Why challenge ye our hearing? And what plea

Put forward, that the sentence of our will

And the Ten's mandate should not be enforc'd?

Isot. Illustrious Prince! And ye, exalted Signors!

'T were hard, even in a presence less august,

To speak of matters, which to merely intimate

Throws doubt upon our virtue: but the safety

Of our lov'd husbands, and our own dear honor,

Therewith involv'd, allow of no reserve.

I know not by what influence, certainly not

Through her enticement, who was ever grave

And decorous in her carriage, my staid lord

Made love to Monna Lutia, while to me

Her gayer mate paid, almost at one time,

A similar compliment. How this should chance

I cannot say. Perhaps being learn'd, they had read,

Like pairs with like, and birds will flock together

VOL. IV.—11

Who find a semblance in each other's feather.
The assembly smile, while ANSELMO
(*on whom* ISOTTA *glances maliciously*) *and* GIROLAMO *mutter
together and exchange looks of rage and shame.*
    Lutia and I from childhood have been friends,
Having had one foster-mother. From the love
We bore our husbands — how reciprocated,
Your Highness has just heard, — we never pass'd,
After our marriage, through each other's door,
Contented o'er a hedge, which parts in two
The garden of our homes, from time to time
To hold communion. Thus it was, one day,
We told each other of our Christian lords,
Who, hating one another unto death,
Kept all their charity for each other's wives:
Again the glance by ISOTTA; *and again* ANSELMO *and*
      GIROLAMO *appear excited.*
And who had grown so curious to explore
Their neighbor's dwelling, that they could not wait
Till Time should open them the common gate,
But sought to creep in by a private door.
*   This time* ANSELMO *and* GIROLAMO —
*especially the latter — are so far mastered by
their passion, that the* CAPTAIN *of the Guard is obliged
to restrain them.* MOCENIGO, *observing the com-
motion, exchanges glances with the Council, and then looks up to the* DOGE,
who thereupon.
Doge. The prisoners will have patience till their hour

To give response.   Else bear them to their cells. —
Proceed, fair lady; nor restrain your wit.

Isot.   To know them better, and to make them know
Us better, and to punish each her spouse,
We plotted to encourage them, and made
Appointments, feigning unto each our lords
Were gone from home; and ere the appointed hour
Each by assistance of the other's maid
Stole to the other's chamber, there awhile
Study'd, and for a purpose, all it held,
Then waited, in the dark as was agreed,
Our husband-lovers.   These had been prepar'd,
For reasons obvious, not to hear us speak.
Our ears however open, while we listen
Each to the worship paid her rival friend,
Sudden there is a tramp upon the stair,
The door is open'd, the attending maid
Warns us of danger, and, still in the dark,
We flee through the garden and regain our homes.
Here stand our maids, the witnesses of all,
And aidant in the plot from first to last. —
What follows need I tell?   The Husband-Lovers,
Detected ignominiously, assum'd
The guilt of a murder which they knew not yet
Had never been committed and had never
Been even attempted, eager to escape
Contempt and laughter in the unconscious grave.

Thus ends our story.   If I have been long,
Weighing on solemn hours, already heavy

With bnrdens of the State, I pray my Prince
And all your Excellencies, for my sex's weakness,
To escape your censure.

    Doge. Nay, receive our praise.
Lady, you have well spoken. What have ye,
Messeri, to respond.

    Ansel. But briefly this:
The story is collusion.

    Isot. And our maids?
Ansel. Are purchas'd.

    Isot. Whence this ring? — Illustrious Prince,
I took it from his finger, in the chamber.
Ansel. 'T was Lntia took it; and thou hadst it thence.
Isot. Here is the copy of the note thou hadst.
I wrote it first for Lutia..

    Girol. 'T is a copy
Perhaps taken after.

    Isot. Say'st thou, Messer Bembo?
My maid will find the woman, an' thou list,
Who took from her the copy, which she bore
From Lutia to Anselmo.

    Ansel. That is nought.
Who cannot buy such women, when thy maid
Herself is pnrchas'd?

    Doge. Messer Barbadico,
Ourself can urge thee. Seest thou nothing, then,
In the dark chamber and the silent lips?
Ansel. Pardon, my liege, — I see no proof therein
Of more than simple shyness, or, be 't said

With greater aptness, merely simple shame.

Girol. [who has been absorbed in thought — suddenly.

But I, magnanimous Prince, begging pardon too
Of all that hear me, plead now for our wives,
Advancing this strong proof.   When she I thought
Was Monna Isotta heard me call her thus,
She drew her hand away, and fell to weeping.
Even then, before I well could think, the alarm
Was given, and the dame escap'd.   But now,
I know 't was Lutia; and I ask forgiveness.

Doge. She is weeping now; but not, I think, from grief.—
And thou, Anselmo, hast thou nought to say?

A pause, ANSELMO *appearing to consider.*

Chapl. [low to Surgeons.

St. Zachary! is he dumb before the Duke!
Wait till I 'm asked: I will not hold my tongue.

Ansel. A light breaks on me too; and I avow,
With penitence, great Duke, we both have sinn'd;
Sinn'd in false censure, as in bad intent.
I do remember now, that I was shock'd,
When fancied Lutia slily laugh'd to hear
My whisper'd vows.   Isotta so had done.

Isot. Yea verily, and did.   And is that all
Thy memory owns?   Thou hast forgot to speak
Of one thing more.   How when I fled away,
I lent thee with my fingers on thy cheek
A compliment which Lutia would not pay.

Ansel. I own the debt, and that 't was well incurr'd.

Doge. These noble ladies' honor is now purg'd

Before all Venice. But not yet absolv'd
Stand their two lords. Rise up, Madonna Mora,
And what thou knowest deliver unreserv'd.

> GISMONDA *rises with an effort, seems to*
> *struggle with herself, then sits down again — or rather*
> *sinks into the chair.*

Chapl. [*in under tone to* 1st *Sur.*

St. Lazarus! poor thing, how scar'd she is!
I should be too. But I am getting old.
Doge. Be not dishearten'd, noble and gentle lady!
Giul. [*low to* Gism.

For Messer Aloise's sake. Madonna,
He would have died for you.

> GISMONDA, *rising instantly, casts one look*
> *on* ALOISE, *then seeming to gather courage, speaks,*
> *with a voice which gradually strengthens in its tone of modest*
> *firmness, but with eyes cast down.*

> *Gism.* It is most true:

He would have died for me. — Illustrious Prince,
Were it my honor, as it is but pride
And womanly shame that are involv'd, — for him,
Who ventur'd life and honor both for me,
Should I not offer it? [*Lifts her eyes with an expres-*
> *sion of deep gratitude to Alo., then casts them*
> *down again. Brief pause.*

> Aloise Foscari

Lov'd me — and woo'd me. But his sire had chosen
Another partner for him. For this cause,

And being of kindred to the Loredani,
My sire forbade me to receive his visits,
Under the certain pain of being shut out
From his heart alike and home.   What could I do?
That very day, Aloise was to come. —
Intercepted by my maid, not knowing why
My father had forbid him, in despair
He urg'd me through the girl to give him hearing
In secret and by night.   As 't was to be
In a balcony, and my maid beside,
The eloquence of his passionate distress,
Repeated by the girl, o'ercame all fear,
And womanly shame, and prudence, and, oh me!
All filial reverence. — At midnight then,
A cord let down drew up to the balcony
A ladder, which we fasten'd to the rail. —
Young Foscaro ascended. [*Her voice breaks.*

                    In his haste
To reach — to reach my outstretch'd arms — he fell.
          Overcome.   Brief pause.

Chapl. [*low.*

     Oh horror! and all saints! he was no robber.
The Duke won't need my evidence after all!

Gism. [*recovering — and with energy.*

     My lord, he is the noblest of all men!
Lest found beneath the window he should stain
Her honor whom he lov'd, he dragg'd away
His body, all broken and bleeding, from the door,
To die elsewhere.

*Pause of brief agitation — looking
tenderly and gratefully on* ALOISE. *The
assembly, with exception of* LOREDANO, *evince deep interest,
and turn their eyes on* ALOISE, *who casts
down his own.*

We saw him, by the moonlight,
Holding his head between his uprais'd hands,
For fear his innocent blood should spot the stones
And be for evidence. — Here is my maid,
Who witness'd all. The ladder is at home. —
To be produc'd, if this be not enough.

The DOGE *bends toward the* COUNSELORS *and the* TEN.
They appear to nod assent.

Doge. It is enough. The prisoner is free.
But did it rest with us, thou noble Gismonda,
He should be bound again with other chains —
Thy heart his prison.
　　　　　Morosini. Rests it then with me?
My daughter Lisa shall not marry now,
My lord, your nephew. He has clomb too high,
And fallen too low.
　　　　　Fosc. So be it. — Aloise. [*with tender
　　　　　　　　reproach.*

Couldst thou not trust me? — Take him, gentle lady;
The gallant boy hast won thee like a hero;
And thou, redeeming him, has shown the prize
Was worth the conquest.

Gism. [*Alo. about to take her hand—*
             looking round to Moro.
But my father ——
    Moro. [*approaching.*] Nay,
I have said, I have no other thought than honor
For Aloise Foscaro; and since
His Procurator sire and Ducal uncle
Sanction the union, I might give my blessing;
But —— [*stops, looking full on Loredano.*
    Lored. What 's 't to me? I stand not in thy way.
Marry thy daughter, man, to whom thou wilt,
Or let her marry herself in thy despite;
That makes me not fourth cousin to the Foscari.
Moro. But it may make thee less of kin to me.
Come hither, children. I have stepp'd between you,
Partly in honor, partly in that, a fool,
I set more by old friendships than new loves.
                    [*Glancing at Loredano.*
I have taught me better now. God bless you both!
Foscaro may be, as thou didst say, Gismonda,
One day the prop of my declining years.
    He puts their hands together. GISMONDA
             raises his to her lips.
Tush, tush! keep all such dainties for thy spouse:
He has better earn'd them.

    While this takes place, the Husband-Lovers
and their wives have embraced. ISOTTA *first extends her hand*
    to ANSELMO, *which he lifts very gravely to kiss;*
    11*

but she draws it away, laughing lightly, and
falls on his neck.

               Doge. All thus endeth well.
And you, Messeri, [*to Ansel. and Girol.*
           we are joy'd to find   .
Are no more foes.   I would your noble example
Might influence others [*glancing at Loredano.*
               to consider friendship
More blest than enmity.
    Lored. [*disdainfully.*] For whom it suits.
Isot. [*low to Ansel., &c.*
I thought it did for every one but brutes.
Doge. Friends, Colleagues, I would thank you one and all.
To your kind sufferance wholly is it owing
This matter is well ended.   It is said,
A shrewd mechanic, somewhere in the North,
Has just devis'd a singular mode to copy
All written labor: so that at one time
A many hundred transcripts may be taken,
In clean fair characters, of a single book. —

A pause ; for the assembly exchange
looks of pleased surprise, or appear to speak briefly togethe
of the matter ; during which

Chapl. [*apart to Sur.*
    Giesu-Maria! it is the Devil's invention !
1st Sur. [*maliciously.*
    They 'll stamp the Bible.
               Chapl. And render all men wise!

1st Sur. The biggest pippin from the tree of knowledge
    Since Adam.
        Chapl. Had it from the sire of lies.
1st Sur. No, from the mother, — as I 've heard it told.
Chapl. 'T is very likely.   But I 'm getting old.
Doge. Nothing shall now be lost to future time.
    This curious story, with its double plot
    And startling mystery, should thus go down
    To entertain posterity like us.
Fosc. Perhaps it may.   And in some far-off time
    Some bard may put the adventures into verse,
    And make a playhouse happy with the scene.
Doge. Then let me tack a moral to the tale.
    To Isot. and Lut.] Deceits are always dangerous, nor
        good ends
    Can ever justify unworthy means.
    To Aloise.] To tell untruth to shield a woman's fame
    May well be generous, as to venture life
    Is at all times heroic; but 't is never
    Either just or virtuous, and is rarely wise.
    The lips may close at will; but, when they open,
    See that they open only for the truth.
Chapl. St. Paul! Our Doge is quite a sage, 't is clear!
Isot. [*to Lut.*] I told you he was Solomon, my dear.
Doge. The College is adjourn'd.

The whole assembly rise, and soon after them the DOGE,
and remain standing.

The main characters, who have already grouped

♦

together, along with the CHAPLAIN, *&c., come now to the*
extreme front of the scene.

Moro. And we, — to meet
Together at my house. [*bowing, though with his rough*
and ungenial manner, to the group.

Girol. To gossip over
The short-liv'd madness of each HUSBAND-LOVER.

Isot. And happy issue of the DOUBLE DECEIT.

Gism. Come with us, Chaplain: you, Messeri, too. [*to Sur.*

Fosc. [*to Chapl.*
To-morrow thou shalt have some work to do.

Chapl. St. Fantin! 't is to make one hand of two.

Fosc. 'T will make at least two happy hearts I pray.

Isot. And so a wedding meetly ends our play."

The Characters draw back, and the
Curtain begins to fall.

Giul. [*advancing, and putting up her hand, as if to stop it.*
Pardon; there should be two.   I claim to see
The brave young spouse your Excellence promis'd me.
[*to Aloise.*

Cass. [*advancing to Girol.*
And I, your Excellence, my triple fee.

Girol. It shall be paid, with interest.

Alo. And some day
My debt to thee, Giulietta.

Giul. Be it now.
'T is time I kept to Giuliet my vow.
Her chaplet fades: 't is long since first I wore

The separate parts.

    Chapl. St. Jude! What can that be?

Giul. A something, Father, which you ne'er before
 I think have seen, and something — to be bold —
 You never, in its parts, I think will see.

Chapl. [*thoughtfully.*

  'T is very likely, child; I 'm getting old.

Gism. Peace, Giulietta: thou art much too free.

Moro. And let the curtain fall; our drama 's o'er.³⁴

Curtain falls.

THE DOUBLE DECEIT

1.—P. 139. THE DOUBLE DECEIT, &c.] The story is founded on the XVth Novel of Bandello.

2.—P. 140. ALOÏSE.] I very much fear that this name would be of but three syllables with an Italian, not merely because *oï* is one of Buommattei's Tuscan diphthongs, but because the Latin form is *Aloysius,* in which the vowels would hardly be separated. In my incertitude, I must beg the favor of the reader to let the diphthong, if it be such in this proper name, remain divided and thus softened (*i* sounded as *e*) into two pure vowel sounds, and ascribe the diæresis to a poetic license which is not unusual in other instances with even the Italians themselves.—In fact, it is little more than anglicizing the name, as is done with *Bianca* (in "Bianca Capello"), which in Italian enunciation would have but two distinct syllables, but with English writers is everywhere of three.*

---

* I take this occasion to observe that perhaps an equal liberty has been taken with *Lutia,* where the accent is laid on the first syllable, although it is

3.—P. 155. —*Cassy!*] Or, "Cassa!" which is more in costume, though not so much in character in the part, in English.

4.—P. 163. *'Drina*—] Contraction of *Cassandrina* (*i* as *e*), the diminutive of familiarity or affection. For the Stage, as more distinctly intelligible, "Wanton", or, as above, "Cassa", or "Candra," both of which are in costume and of the time, in the same way as is *Monna*, contracted from *Madonna*.

5.—P. 164. *I have not*, etc.] Or, "I have not repented that I then gave way" (—"that I gave thee way"); or, "I have not repented to have given thee way."

6.—P. 166. —*to me?*] —"to thee?" if preferred.

7.—P. 166. *As lofty*, etc.] Omit, for the Stage.

8.—P. 166. *Were it*, etc.] Otherwise:

> "Were it the Duke's own son, I might relent,
> But being his brother Marco's, I will not."

Or:

> "Were it the Doge's son, I might relent,
> But being the Procurator's, I will not."

9.—P. 166. *Thy bed is yet a widow's.   Make thy choice.   So he be not*, etc.] Otherwise:

> "Thy bed is yet a widow's. Take thy choice.
> Out of a thousand noble youths, not many
> Would slight Gismonda Mora or her dower."

---

apparently but another form for *Lucia*, which, notwithstanding its Latin derivation, compels in Italian the stress of the voice to fall on *i*. That it is a matter of choice will be evident, from the fact that *An'na*, *Bar'ta*, *Ghet'ta* (contr. of *Arrighetta*, Henrietta), *Le'lia*, *Liv'ia*, *Pau'la*, and some others, would any of them suit the rhythm and the verse.

And in the text, for the last line, may be redd (but the variation is trivial): "Giovanni Moro will not say thee nay," or "John Moro will not say his daughter nay."

10.—P. 167. *If Procurator*, etc.] Otherwise:

> " If Aloise, Marco's son, comes in,
> Gismonda, Niccolo's widow, shall go out."

Or, the three lines may read simply:

> " Do as beseems thee. But of this rest sure ;
> If Aloise enter, thou goest out."

11.—P. 168. *Giulietta !*] The name is properly of three syllables. The reader will please allow the diæresis occasionally, to favor the verse, (although it is really an oversight). In the present instance, might be redd: " What ho, Giulietta." But that were too masculine for *Gismonda*.— See, in Note 2, the remark on *Bianca*.

12.—P. 171. *The women's rooms are in the hinder part, Divided from the men's.*] See SCAMOZZI. *L'Idea dell' Architett. Univ.* P. I. L. III. c. 6. p. 243. (*Venet.* in fol. 1615.) Established in Venice, where or in whose environs his chief works were executed, the famous architect took pleasure in comparing, in his elaborate work, this domestic arrangement with that of the ancient Greeks.

13.—P. 173. *— balcónies —*] Throughout the piece, I have, against my will, adopted for the word *balcony* the accentuation of Walker; which is that used by Byron, and by the older poets. I have done this, because I do not know but that it still obtains in England, and therefore is the received accentuation of the Stage. Yet in this country, I have never heard it (except from the lips of a South-American Spaniard) pronounced otherwise than *bal'cony*, which is the pronunciation that must eventually prevail, even on the Stage, because *balco'ny* is contrary to the genius of our language and therefore difficult of enunciation when in connection with purely English words.— *January* 23, 1856.

14.—P. 173. — *Cà* —] Familiar Venetian contraction for *Casa*, indicating the mansion or palace of families of distinction. *Casa Veniero* is merely the mansion of the Venieri family, which for the sake of costume, that is of better localizing the scene and adding to 'ts semblance of verity, is feigned to be in the immediate neighbor-hood of the "Casa Mora." *Cà Ziani* — *Cà Priuli* — *Cà Micheli* are all varieties of reading in the MS.

15.—P. 173. — *when St. Mark tolls four* —] The reader will allow me to remind him here of the peculiarity in the notation of Italian time, which is counted, for the twenty-four hours, from sunset to sunset. "About the fourth. 'T will then be midnight," as above, places of course the scene in midsummer, like the men-tion of San Vito's day in the beginning of the next *Act.*

16.—P. 181. St. Teddy's —] Or, "St. Theodore's." The pillar is one of the famous two (See scene-description, *Act. I.*, *Sc.* 2) which have the ominous *Intercolonnio* alluded to in *Act V.*, *Sc.* 4; where See Note 29.

17.—P. 184. *St. Moses!*] The Venetians canonize *Moses, Job*, and other sanctities of the Old Testament, and have churches erected to them, while the theatres in the neighborhood take their names from the churches ; so that there is, or was, a *Theatre of St. Moses*, of *St. Samuel*, etc., as well as of *St. Luke.* See WRIGHT'S *Observations in Travelling, &c.*, 2d ed. (Lond. 1764, in 4to.) pp. 61, 84.

18.—P. 184. *I'll strip the other off*, etc.] Otherwise, to avoid the double accentuation in "St. Giu'liet'", which is but a metrical license (though only too common a one in English):

" I 'll strip its fellow off, and make the pair
A chaplet for my patron-saint to wear."

And above :

———— " Never mind ;
As well a leg-band as another kind,
To noose [snare — ensnare] a husband."——

19.—P. 185. — 'T is Holy Vito's day.] When a solemn pro-
cession, which included the Doge himself, was always made to the
Church of the Saint, in acknowledgment of the defeat of Bajamonte
Tiepolo's conspiracy, which occurred on that day (*June* 15, 1310),
or on the previous night. See MARIN SANUTO. *Vit. Duc. Venet.* ap.
MURATOR. *Rer. Ital. Script.* XXII. (*Mediol.* 1733, *in fol.*) col. 585, 6.—
It was on the occasion of this conspiracy that the formidable
Council of the Ten was instituted. *ib.* 586.— The anniversary was
still observed in Edw. Wright's day (four hundred years after-
ward). *Obs. &c.,* as above, p. 58.

20.—P. 191. *Gismonda !* Gism. *O God ! he has fallen ! he is
dead !* Giul. *Hush, hush !*] This verse is not redundant. The *a*
of "Gismonda", being unaccented, slides easily into the succeeding
unemphatic *O*, without combining with it, a not ungraceful and a
convenient usage frequent enough in English poetry, especially
with Milton ; and "has" and "is" are slurred, as is common at all
times with these auxiliaries where not emphasized.

Gismon' | da̅ O̅ God' | he has fall'n | he is dead' | hush, hush

The variation does not arise from necessity. Besides the alterations
that obviously might be made in the verse itself, the whole passage
as originally written stood thus:

Gism. He pulls upon it to try.— He is on it now !
He mounts ! — He is half way up ! — O God ! he has fallen !
[*with anguish, yet in a suppressed tone.*
She retreats from the window.
He is dead !

Giul. Hush, hush, Madonna! 't may not be.
[*Beckons her to the balcony, over which
Giulietta is looking.*
Look! he is moving; he is not hurt. He holds
Both hands to his head. Look; now your eyes are us'd, *etc.*

21.—P. 202. — *quite* —] I take pleasure in repeating here this word (or form of a word), which I would gladly revive. (See, on p. 135, Note 1.) If it be objected to, it is easy for the Stage to substitute "pay," or, for that matter, "quit."

22.—P. 205. No, 't is not very amiable.—] Or, "No, 't is more strong than amiable." Or, again, "No, 't is more pertinent than nice." The choice is with the Stage.

23.—P. 205. *Of every Pantaloon.*] That is, *Venetian gentleman.* The origin of the word, whence our *Pantaloon* (WEBSTER, with his absurdly-mongrel conjectural derivation, to the contrary notwithstanding,) is said, with great plausibility, to be *Piantar leone* (*plant* (fix) *the lion*), in allusion to the arms of Venice. In Italian, *Pantalone* is a masque representing a Venetian ("spezie di maschera rappresentante il Veneziano.") The Academy cites Michelangelo Buonaroti (the Younger) in *La Fiera.*

24.—P. 206. *It cost me dear then. It was devilish bitter,* etc.] Or, "Pleasantry in my mouth — but devilish bitter, *etc.*"

25.—P. 208. — *Rather damn ourselves,* etc.] Or, if preferred, though it is not so characteristic in the situation:

"Rather our own folly,
To fancy that we trod on solid ground,
While grinning at our neighbor's floor of glass."

The Stage sometimes strains at gnats, and *damn* in such a place (since thrice repeated) might be one of them.

26.—P. 210. —*what was perilous to reveal.*] Perhaps, considering the reason why *Aloise* uttered the cry, as indicated by the
exclamation below, "O fatal slip!" (i. v. of the lips, as respected
Gismonda's secret,) it might be better to read, —"what he gladly
would conceal."

27.—P. 210. *I did.* —*O fatal slip!* etc.] Otherwise, and more
directly intelligible, but not so characteristic, nor so elevated in
language:

> "Did I?—Unhappy error!
>> 1*st Sur.* Said I right?"

28.—P. 220. Lored. (muttered.) *It yet may be.*] The misfortunes
of the Foscari and the implacable hatred of the Loredani are well
known to the readers of Byron.—It may be of interest to subjoin
the following news-item cut from one of our journals a year after
the composition of this drama. The *Double Deceit* was written,
1855–6, (*Dec.* 4, 1855—*Jan.* 21, 1856); the scrap is marked in the
margin simply 1856–7.

"In one of his letters from Venice, M. von Hacklander says that the illustrious family of the Foscaris is extinct. A few years ago two old ladies of the
name inhabited a small room in the family palace, and the last male scion of
the Foscaris not long since died as an inferior member of a traveling histrionic
company."

29.—P. 234. Take care of the columns!] A Venetian proverb
and local superstition. *Guardatevi del intercolonnio!* "Beware of
the space between the columns!"—because of the purpose to
which anciently the place was put, viz. the beheading of criminals.
Marin Faliero, when elected Doge, being unable to land at the
usual place because of the tide, was forced to pass between the
pillars. And the people remembered the omen, when he was after-
wards beheaded.   .

30.—P. 235. *I wish I had them bound upon a plank*, etc.] Said
to be the mode of drowning criminals.

31.—P. 239. (*which from its private nature*, etc.)] The whole of
this parenthesis to be omitted on the Stage.

32.—P. 251. *Either just or*, etc.] The present received pronunciation of *either* may make it advisable to substitute "Or just or,
etc."

33.—P. 252. *And so a wedding meetly ends our play.*] Here the
Curtain may fall. All that follows is an addition made subsequently
(January 22) to this, the original conclusion of the piece, and may
by a caviling disposition be considered impertinent. It was made,
to give *Giulietta* and *Cassandra*, who are really important and
pleasant characters in the drama, an opportunity to say their say.
The most serious objection to it (to me, but not to the Stage, which
scarcely knows what verisimilitude or what nature is in our English
drama) is on the score of probability. The parties would hardly
remain in presence of the Senate, to gratify two saucy waiting-
maids, even if these were likely to retain their smartness on such
an occasion. The option, to admit or to reject, is with the Theatre.

34.—P. 253. *'Tis very likely, child;* etc.] Or, omitting *Gismon-*
da's part:

> *Chapl.* 'T is very likely, child; I am getting old.
> *Moro.* Come, drop the baize; our business here is o'er.

NOTICE

THE two pieces here presented are of a series of nineteen, which it is proposed to collect into four or five volumes, and the whole of which, with two exceptions, are completed and ready for the press; namely:

Calvary; *Virginia*; *Bianca Capello*; *Ugo da Este*; *Uberto*; *The Last Mandeville*; *Matilda of Denmark*; *Meleager*; *Palamedes*; *Œnone*; *Pyrrhus, Son of Achilles*; *Don Sancho Ortiz.* Tragedies.

The Silver Head; *The Double Deceit*; *The Montanini*; *The Magnetizer*; *The Prodigal*; *The Double-dealer*; *The Dead Alive.* Comedies.

The first two on the list have recently been published. The next to appear will be *Bianca Capello* and *Ugo da Este*, forming with *Calvary* and *Virginia* the First Volume of Tragedies.

www.ingramcontent.com/pod-product-compliance
Lightning Source LLC
Chambersburg PA
CBHW020357030726
47496CB00007B/2175

9783744791960